Top Secret

Captain Eric H. Swenson

PublishAmerica
Baltimore

© 2004 by Eric H. Swenson.
All rights reserved. No part of this book may be reproduced, stored in a retrieval system or transmitted in any form or by any means without the prior written permission of the publishers, except by a reviewer who may quote brief passages in a review to be printed in a newspaper, magazine or journal.

First printing

ISBN: 1-4137-3115-5
PUBLISHED BY PUBLISHAMERICA, LLLP
www.publishamerica.com
Baltimore

Printed in the United States of America

10/22/04

To Sven,
with best wishes

Capt Eric Swenson

TABLE OF CONTENTS

Acknowledgments	7
Foreword	9
Prologue	13
Chapter I: The Gathering	19
Chapter II: In The Beginning	36
Chapter III: Whom Shall We Send	50
Chapter IV: Underway	64
Chapter V: On Station	81
Chapter VI: Give Us This Day	97
Chapter VII: The Exodus	116
Chapter VIII: Do Not Look Back	127
Chapter IX: This Too Shall Pass	139
Chapter X: Remember The Sabbath	151
Chapter XI: The Scattering	164
Epilogue	179
Appendix I	181
Appendix II	182
Glossary of Terms	183

Acknowledgments

My first acknowledgment must be to my wife Nancy who after years of hearing me tell my stories, persuaded me to start putting my tales on paper.

Secondly, my friend and most helpful critic Bob Zilm of Soquel, California. Bob and I worked together on the Peacekeeper Canister program at Westinghouse Electric Corporation's Marine Division. Bob's continued constructive comments reassured me that I was on the right track and kept me going.

My submarine friend and shipmate, Lt. Larry Coleman, USN (ret.) who helped me immeasurably with many of the technical details of the operational phases of my story. Captain Benjamin Campbell Jarvis USN (ret.) helped me correct some of the facts as presented.

I also wish to thank the "Prime Timer's" writing group at California State University Chico for their patience in listening to my various episodes of this story and their very astute questions about submarine life and operations. I didn't consider any of this group as the audience I was writing for and that in itself was stimulating, helping me to retain my mental frame of mind and not wavering on the road to getting the story published. One member of the writing group, John Coverdale, helped steer me into making my writing more readable.

My daughter, an English teacher, and my son both urged me to continue the story because they wanted to "hear more."

My gratitude extends beyond the mechanics and motivation of

my friends but goes to the officers of the United States Navy's submarine force that were such fine shipmates and teachers that enabled me to qualify in submarines and later achieve five commands. The guidance of top notch Naval Academy officers, two of whom were promoted to the rank of Vice Admiral, were most helpful and motivated me to achieve all I could while on active duty in the Navy as well as in the Naval Reserve

Photo Credits:

U.S. Navy
U.S. Submarine Force Library
U.S. Naval Institute
Royal Hawaiian Hotel

Foreword

This tale about the *U.S.S. Dolphin* (SS-169) is intended to honor the brave officers and men who served aboard this submarine from commissioning to scrapping. Their courage in taking this pioneer submarine to sea, let alone on war patrol, was of the highest order.

While the incidents in this story really happened they didn't necessarily occur to the venerable old *Dolphin*. Many of these events occurred to *Dolphin* but not in the time frame depicted. To avoid embarrassment or concern of any of the officers or men who were aboard her during the time I am writing about, I have taken great pains to use fictitious names and descriptions.

In part, this story has its roots in the fact that President Roosevelt ordered three small sailing vessels, obviously armed, sent into Japanese territory near the Indonesian Islands prior to December 7, 1941. These three ships were sent on their missions in an attempt to discover what the Japanese objectives really were. The fact that these sailing ships were commissioned, armed and deployed indicates the United States government was well aware that the Japanese were up to something. Perhaps my story about the *Dolphin* could have been true. Who knows?

Kagoshima Wan, situated at the most southwesterly tip of the island of Kyushu, is the scene of action for this story. This area is the province of Japan where the flag of the Empire of Japan derived its flag. A white banner with a red ball in the center. It was the flag of the independent province before Japan was unified as an Empire.

My memories of the early submarines that I was privileged to serve aboard are very vivid and I look back on them fondly. Many of those early submarines should never have been sent into combat if it weren't for the dire, brutal necessity of taking the war to the Japanese immediately after their attack on the United Sates of America at Pearl Harbor.

My memories to this day are as vivid as the day they occurred. The smell of mineral spirits used to wipe down the internal brass piping and equipment in order to control corrosion still lingers in my mind as well as the cramped but orderly conditions below decks as well as top side. I was in awe of the sailors that I saw standing their watch or refurbishing some equipment. Their appearance alone seemed to tell me that I made the correct decision in wanting to be a submariner.

It never occurred to me that the submarine on the surface was so fragile and so easily sunk. I read all of Commander Edward Ellsberg's books which covered submarine disasters in the early days but I was still not deterred from becoming a submarine sailor.

Many of the events I wrote about in *Top Secret* I personally experienced aboard the *USS Snapper (SS - 185)* during World War II and others I learned about through discussions with many of my shipmates in the "Submarine Veterans of World War II" organization. Some of the events bring back some memories that are disturbing but many are humorous and heart warming. My intention is to pay homage to my former shipmates who have passed on and I dedicate my efforts in my writing to their families and descendants.

All submariners owe a lot to those who pioneered in the older undersea boats. Many of these old timers were lost when their boats were sunk or in some cases when they were washed overboard from the narrow decks and exposed bridge structures. Submarining is a complex and dangerous business. Submarines perform many different tasks. Among those tasks are: Photo reconnaissance, mine laying, torpedoing ships, charting waters, shore bombardment, inserting guerila troops behind enemy lines, evacuating surrounded personnel and many more operations. All of these tasks can be performed far more efficiently by surface ships, aircraft, PT boats, destroyers and mine layers. Then, why is it that a submarine was employed to do these things? In a word "secrecy." When a submarine leaves port and submerges, hopefully, no body knows where it is going or what task it has been assigned to perform. In some cases submarines were loaded with foul weather gear when in fact they were heading into a tropical region in order to convey to any enemy agents a contrary objective. These were some of the reasons that the Submarine Force has been labeled the Silent Service.

In 1938 the *San Francisco Examiner* had a section headlined by the statement: "Hawaii – Our Greatest Defense Outpost."

The article went on to say that, "The Pearl Harbor Navy base on Oahu was the most-guarded port under the American flag." It was described as "America's Gibralter of the Pacific." The Army's $2 million ammunition depot contained more than $20 million worth of bombs, shells, and cartridges. It continued by describing the fortifications and mechanized units manned by 20,000 troops supported by fighting planes and long range bombers. The article further stated that: The entire American fleet can be concentrated in Pearl Harbor."

The entire population of Oahu at that time was 380,000 civilians of which 150,000, a little less than half, were Japanese. Of the Japanese, 35,000 were still aliens with the remainder being citizens by birth or by agreement when the United States took over the islands as a territory. The rationalization for our adopting the Hawaiian Islands as a territory was the fact that, under the control of a foreign nation, bombers and ships could launch attacks directly at the United States' West coast. As the keystone of our Pacific strategy, Hawaii stands guard over our western border. The article further stated that: "Hawaii is no threat to other nations, whose distances from Hawaii exceed the practical limits of offensive action. Hawaii is not an offensive base, but a fundamental necessity of our national defense."

On the same page was an article about the Japanese crushing all competition. The lead paragraph stated: "While Japanese goodwill missions tour the United States to convince the American people of the friendship and brotherly love of Japan for this country, the campaign goes ruthlessly on in Tokyo to freeze out every American industry operating in the Land of the Rising Sun." Their primary efforts were toward the American automobile business. The Japanese army demanded that their government manufacture cars and trucks for the military purposes of mobilization and supply, and not be dependent on American imports that could be suddenly cut off in time of emergency. (Did they mean "in time of war?")

In addition the Japanese conducting goodwill tours around the United States they were providing low-cost steamship transportation to and from Japan in order to demonstrate how open their country had become. All the tours were specifically designed to show a peaceful Japan. Little did we know that behind the scenes the Japanese were rapidly preparing for war with the United States of America.

Prologue

The United States Navy struggled with submarine design up through the 1930s. The first designs were single hull with internal ballast tanks and were powered by gasoline engines. The gasoline engines were dangerous and emitted toxic fumes. There were many cases of explosions, fires, and personnel overcome by fumes. Gasoline engines were no longer used in our submarines after 1912. The Navy used German U-Boats that we had received as reparations at the end of World War I to determine what they did that was so effective for them that we didn't know about. Some of our earlier boats resembled the U-Boats.

Basic design went from single hull construction to double hull and then finally settled on a combination of both which we employed through out World War II. An excellent treatise on the evolution of U.S. submarine design can be found in, *The Fleet Submarine in the U.S. Navy*, by Commander John D. Alden U.S. Navy (ret.) published by the Naval Institute Press.

In 1916 the US Navy began an experiment with nine **V** class submarines which proved to be little more than just that. An experiment. It resulted in a long list of design features which were ordered *not* to be repeated but some critical beneficial ones were incorporated in future designs. The V-1, V-2 and V-3, the Barracuda, Bass, and Bonita were the worst of the lot and never served in a combat capacity to the best of my knowledge. They were very unhandy on the surface as well as being very wet and uncomfortable.

The shark like nose of this class would plow into the oncoming waves instead of riding up over them. A shipmate of mine, a former crew member of the Bass, said, "Each and every dive was a new adventure." He told me that he was sure glad he wasn't a Quartermaster then and had to stand watches on **that** extremely wet bridge because it was practically under water all the time when on the surface.

V-4, The *Argonaut* at 381 feet in length was the largest US submarine built until the nuclear powered *Triton* (SSN-586) was launched in 1959. *Argonaut* was specifically designed for mine laying but was never used as a minelayer to my knowledge. She was unwieldy and difficult to control at high submerged speeds and steep angles. V-4 was sunk by the Japanese in January 1943 while performing war patrol duties for which she was ill-suited to accomplish.

V-5 and V-6, the *Narwhal* and *Nautilus* were 11 feet shorter with no mine laying capabilities like the V-4 but similar to the V-4, were very clumsy and awkward submarines. A popular saying among submarine sailors: "Blow, Back, and Pray," described the extreme difficulty with which the V-4, V-5, and V-6 had in recovering from steep dives. Try pushing a 1 x 12 plank through the water sideways and you will soon get the idea of how difficult these submarines were to operate submerged, especially pulling out of steep dives. Despite that handicap the V-5 and the V-6 of the three "Big Boats" performed valiant service during World War II, but not in the capacity for which they were designed.

Dolphin D-1 circa 1934

V-7, the *Dolphin,* was designed as a long-range cruiser type submarines. The designation was later changed to D-1 and then to SS-169. *Dolphin* at 370 feet, incorporated all of the best features of the previous V boats and shed most of the detrimental features but retained riveted construction since welding had not yet been deemed to be satisfactory for submarine construction. The reduction of construction costs of the V-7, primarily through weight loss, were significant and the basic design turned out to be very serviceable and essentially became the prototype of the fleet type submarine designed for long range patrol operations that was used throughout WWII.

V-8 and V-9, the *Cachalot* and *Cuttlefish* were the last of the "V" boats and were relatively successful. The *Cuttlefish,* I believe, enjoyed the distinction of being the first submarine that incorporated welded hull construction. The principle draw back of these two boats was they were limited in speed and endurance or range. The succeeding "Fleet Boats" had greater fuel capacity and, thanks to the introduction of air conditioning, became much more habitable. They also had better diesel engines and ultimately all of our wartime submarines were propelled by diesel-electric power. That is the diesels were connected to generators that could either drive the propulsion motors while on the surface or charge the batteries or both.

The U.S. Navy's submarines, despite their numerous draw backs, were the most habitable of all the submarines of all the navies in the world. They had air-conditioning and good, but not adequate enough, fresh provisions storage and excellent meals were generally served to the crews. The submarine cooks did a marvelous job in preparing the meals under very difficult conditions. Berthing for the officers and enlisted men was generally cramped. Despite the cramped conditions, "hot bunking" where a sailor came off watch and crawled in the bunk of a man going on watch, was relatively rare. There were, indeed, times when as many as 60 refugees or other military personnel were taken aboard and transported to a safe haven. Space was then at a premium.

The Naval shipyards that built submarines at the onset of World War II were Portsmouth Naval Shipyard at Portsmouth, New Hampshire; Electric Boat Company at Groton, Connecticut; and Mare Island Naval Shipyard at Vallejo, California. In order to increase production early on during the war, Manitowoc Shipbuilding Company, Manitowoc, Wisconsin and Cramp Shipbuilding Company of Philadelphia, Pennsylvania, were brought into the picture. Manitowoc built their submarines according to Electric Boat Company plans for the most part and the Cramp yard followed Portsmouth plans; however Cramp seemed to be unable to build submarines and was constantly bogged down with various construction difficulties. Some of the keels that were laid down by Cramp were towed as completed hulls to Portsmouth Naval Shipyard where they were finished, and commissioned. One Cramp yard submarine, the *USS Sabalo (SS-302)* for example, took approximately one year from keel laying to launching and another year from launching to commissioning. That was a relatively rare example of production rates.

TOP SECRET

Another would be the *USS Snook (SS-279)* which took six months and seven days from keel laying to commissioning. This was one of the shortest submarine fabrications of the war. We will be unable to match that kind of production rate in the future with our current nuclear production techniques.

All of the submarines commissioned up until the later part of 1942 had the prewar type conning tower fairwater. There was a steering stand and wheel located in the forward part of the bridge and the enclosure, including portholes, added to an already bulky profile. Shortly after hostilities began, the forces afloat began reducing the silhouette as much as possible. Eliminating the bridge steering and erecting a twenty millimeter gun platform in its place helped lower the submarine's silhouette and at the same time provided a small measure of defense. At the same time, the then enclosed "cigarette deck" at the after end of the bridge was opened up to reduce or lower the ships profile still further. The cigarette deck also sported a twenty millimeter gun. By late 1942 the production yards were creating the new lower profiles the operating submarines required.

Armament, at first, consisted of four 21-inch torpedo tubes fore and aft and by late 1939 was increased to six tubes in the bow and four in the stern. The later arrangements were to be continued throughout the war. The main deck gun started out as a 3-inch 50 caliber dual purpose, later changed as the war progressed, to a 4-inch 50 caliber single purpose and then 5-inch 25 caliber dual purpose weapons. Other armament consisted of 30 and 50 caliber machine guns later increased to 20 mm and 40 mm guns as they were found to be adaptable for submarine use. This increase in armament occurred as the war grew to a close and targets were reduced to small sea going ships. Many higher ranking officers did not want deck weapons because a submarine is so easily sunk, when on the surface, by the enemy's weapons. They wanted commanding officers to keep the submarine submerged and exposed for the shortest possible time.

Radar for submarines first appeared on the *USS Gar (SS-206)* in mid 1941. It was called the SD radar. Its use was to enable the submarine to detect radar. Its fixed antenna had first been designed for radio transmitting and was adapted for radar use. It was omnidirectional and it was later found that the Japanese could home in on the radiations. Japanese aircraft could be seen on the horizon and they would disappear from sight and radar and then suddenly show up a few miles away heading in low and fast. By the end of the war submarines had various radars for surface and aerial search and finally an excellent radar that was incorporated into the larger of the two periscopes.

Color schemes varied from light Navy gray or white to black at the start of the war but in general from the overhead looking down flat surfaces were painted dull black. From the profile point of view the hull and superstructure were frequently painted with differing shades of gray deepening from light at the bow to dark at the stern. Some mottling effects were sometimes used.

The life's blood of these submarines was diesel oil. On December 7, 1941, the Japanese fortunately failed to bomb the Navy's diesel oil tank farm above the submarine base. Had they destroyed the oil supply we may not have been able to send our submarines on extended patrols for some time.

The Naval shipyards as well as civilian yards made extraordinary progress in modernizing the submarines coming in from patrol and bringing them up to current standards. As each boat returned from a war patrol their patrol reports were analyzed. The operating forces made suggestions about changes in configuration, from time to time, and these were implemented. The result was that no two submarines, even sisters ships from the same yard, were identical. Many of these changes were passed on to construction yards. Consequently the newly arriving boats had a silhouettes much different than their predecessors.

Chapter I: The Gathering

    I hailed a cab at Honolulu International Airport and headed into the city of Honolulu. It was a pleasant ride and I enjoyed the balmy atmosphere as we drove along familiar territory. A glimpse of the billowing, glowing white, cumulus clouds trying to crowd their way through the Pali Pass highway over to Kailua was a pleasant reminder of my once tranquil life on Oahu. Once within the city limits I had the driver stop at a small florist's shop. The aroma from various blossoms was almost intoxicating. The little shop had a vibrant display of colorful leis in front but my mission was not to buy a lei. The airline had already placed one around my neck. My purpose was to purchase a small wreath. Getting back into the cab my trip continued. At my direction we took a left turn on Punchbowl Street.
    A few blocks later I directed the driver to pull into a small cemetery. I stopped at the small office by the gate and asked about my bill. The cab driver then drove me to a small corner of the lush landscaped grounds. Locating the grave, I knelt and placed the wreath on top of the little stone marker. I said a little prayer. I stood up, paused in thought for a moment, came back to reality and got into the cab. The driver was smart enough to not ask me any questions as I stowed my emotions in that special part of my brain that I do not dip into very often..
    I was ambivalent about attending the Submarine Veteran's Convention being held in Honolulu. Part of me didn't want to resurface some sad old memories I had of Honolulu. Another part of me wanted to visit the submarine base at Pearl Harbor where I spent so many years of my life. I was appointed to my first submarine

command at that base during the Vietnam war. I'm proud of that so the choice was easy. The sadness will always be there. The taxi dropped me off in front of my hotel.

It was with much trepidation that I entered the venerable lobby of that famous old hotel, the Royal Hawaiian. The Royal was built by the Matson Navigation Company in 1927 and had 400 rooms. Tourism was starting to grow but was effectively stopped by the stock market crash of 1929. The hotel was well remembered by the hundreds of submarine sailors who spent two weeks of R & R. in those rooms following a war patrol in the Pacific during World War II. My heart was pounding as I went up to the registration desk. I'm sure my blood pressure must have shot up as I stared at the majestic old structure with its high ceilings and pink colored walls.

At one time the Royal Hawaiian was a magnificent hotel on Wakiki beach along with the only other hotel, the Ala Moana. They were the only two hotels on the beach at that time. But by 1998 the Royal squatted like a pink colored midget amongst the multitude of high rise tourist hotels.

The Royal Hawaiian

A sharp slap on the back broke my reverie.

"Hey, Captain! How goes it? Long time no see."

Turning, I looked into the smiling face and piercing blue eyes of Carl Braun. Braun was an Engineman on the *Blackfin* when I was aboard her in 1951. Square-jawed and muscular, he had the same physique he had during the *Blackfin's* WestPac patrol in '52, though his hair was now graying and showing a receding hairline.

"Carl!"

We shook hands for what seemed an eternity. A tear started to form in my eyes and I thought I noticed the same sort of watering in Carl's eyes.

"Nice to see you. You look like you're still in pretty good shape."

"Thanks, Captain! I still feel like I could hold my own aboard a boat today. Come on, let's get you settled in."

Speechless, I watched as he effortlessly hefted my suitcase and carry on bag and placed them on the cart provided by the hotel. Next he firmly escorted me over to the registration desk. After registration, Carl quickly tipped and dismissed the bell-hop who was standing waiting to help. He then ensconced me and my bags in a third floor room with a panoramic view of the ocean and beach. I pleasantly thought of sitting there and enjoying the view. But it seemed Carl had other thoughts.

"Sir, if you're not too beat let's get down to the check-in desk and get your package of goodies and your name tag. I'm sure that there'll be a lot of guys there that'll want to see you and you'll want to see them, too. Let's go."

"Carl, you're something else. I need to relax and I would like to settle down a bit and could also use a drink."

"OK, Captain. My room is on this floor too. We can hoist one there before we sign you in."

"Let's go."

Carl's room, three doors down the hall, was the same configuration as mine and had a view of the ocean and beach also. With no wife to share it, I wondered how much time I would spend looking out the window in my room. Carl opened the small refrigerator and got the ice tray out. No need for the ice machine, wherever that was. He was anxious to talk and to get down to the convention check-in desk. He quickly poured two "'unmeasured" Scotches on the rocks and sat down.

"Captain, I'll never forget the time you spent getting me out of that stupid fiasco with the Shore Patrol that time in San Diego."

"It was just in the line of duty, Carl."

"Yeah but you had to take time away from your wife and kids, didn't you?"

"It didn't take more than a few hours, Carl, and my kids were asleep anyhow."

"You were told to do it, weren't you?"

"I was asked to help out by the executive officer if I could. I said I would. That's all there was to it."

"Well, belated thanks anyway, Captain."

"You're welcome. You always stood by me aboard ship and I know that you covered for me a time or two."

As we chatted he kept crossing his legs, vigorously exercising the upper one giving me the distinct signal that he was anxious to get down stairs to convention headquarters. He was eager to be my guide. I was comfortable with him in that role. I knew that he had been promoted to Master Chief Petty Officer before he retired from the Navy. Fidgety, he obviously couldn't wait to get me down to the convention desk and meet some of the men. So, after that one drink and small talk about some sailors we both knew, we headed down to the convention check-in desk.

There were a number of faces, with bodies attached, milling around the room. Most of them were wearing their traditional blue vests covered with memorabilia from previous conventions. They proudly sported patches on the vests that indicated the boats they served aboard. Some of them were sporting "Digger" hats they had adapted from the time they were based in Australia. A great many of them looked familiar but I couldn't tie a name to any of them. I wasn't wearing the normal vest with my name or boats indicated as most of the veterans had. I wondered who would know or want to see me at this gathering? Braun gave the man at the desk my name and got my package. He took my name tag out of the envelope and slapped it on my chest with a force that almost knocked me over. I guess I must have really needed that tag.

"Hey, Watch it, Carl. I'm not as young as I used to be."

"Sorry, Captain. I'm just trying to help get you started right. You haven't been to one of these conventions before, have you?"

"No I haven't."

"Didn't think so. I thought I'd just show you the ropes and make it a little easier for you."

"That's fine, Carl, but just slow down a bit."

A large scale model of a World War II diesel powered submarine about ten feet long, surrounded by about twenty men or so, occupied an alcove of the room. In another alcove a group of men were clustered around a table looking through some binders.

"What's going on over there, Carl?" I asked, pointing to the fellows leafing through the binders.

"Oh, those are the boat books."

"Boat books?"

"Yeah. Everyone is supposed to sign in on the boats they served on so they can get together for…you know... for whatever, –drinks, dinner– later on. I'll take you over and get you properly signed in."

I momentarily thought back to the eleven submarines that I had served on in various capacities…I wondered if there were any chances that I'd find someone who was on the *Dolphin* with me. I was startled by the yelling of some of the fellows who had apparently found the name of a long lost shipmate. I looked back at the men examining the scale model and made eye contact with one of them. He seemed to recognize me and immediately headed toward us. He looked vaguely familiar to me. As he approached, my memory banks recycled and I made a match. That large cranium with intense eyes under scored by a determined face could only belong to Ltjg Burgess who was with me on the *Diodon* when I was engineering officer. I extended my hand.

"Captain! It's good to see you again."

"Same here, Paul. It's nice to see you too. As I recall you had just made Lieutenant when you left the *Diodon*. Someone later told me that you had resigned your commission."

"You got bum dope on that score, Captain. I didn't resign although I had intended to."

"I lost track of you after you left. What did you end up doing?"

"I decided to go back to college. To help with my expenses I joined the Naval Reserve. There was a Submarine Reserve unit nearby which was convenient."

"That was a good move, Paul. I had my share of two weeks annual training in the Reserve. Did you keep up with the annual training duty requirements?"

"Sure did. Kept my hand in submarines for two weeks Active Duty for Training every year. One year I was able to get in four weeks. Two weeks back-to-back."

"You must have been busy what with work, school and the Navy."

"I was. I never knew time to fly by so fast. I did my studying down in my office in the basement and the two boys used to holler "good night daddy" through the floor furnace each night."

"At least you were there for them when they needed you."

"After serving in various capacities they appointed me commanding officer of my reserve unit. By the time I was eligible for retirement I had been promoted to full Commander"

"Congratulations, Paul."

Braun who had been standing by taking all this in suddenly interrupted:

"Captain, I'm going to see if we can take the sub base tour tomorrow if that's OK with you."

I had become so engrossed in my conversation of an old friend that I had forgotten that Carl was at my side. My face reddened and I turned toward him.

"Carl, I'm sorry. I'd like you to meet Commander Burgess. He was with me on the *Diodon*."

"Glad to meet you, sir."

"My pleasure."

"By your leave, Captain? I'll set up the tour for both of us. OK?"

"Fine, Carl."

Carl was happy to get away from the boring conversation with another guy from another boat and scooted off. I turned back to Paul.

"Which tour was he talking about, Captain?"

"Oh, the general Sub Base tour."

"I'd like to take that one also. I'll sign up for it and maybe we could ride together."

"That'd be fine. We could do some more reminiscing."

"I'm for that."

"Sorry about the interruption, Paul. How are Kathy and the kids? What did you major in?"

"You do remember Kathy, don't you, Captain?"

"I sure do. She was one nice lady and pretty, too."

"Well, she supported my decision to go back to school. She even got a part-time job. We were lucky to have her parents living nearby to look after the two boys while she was working."

"Convenient. How long did that arrangement last?"

"Took all of three years. But it was worth every minute of it. I got my Master's Degree in Public Relations and the kids had a good family life."

"Didn't it take a while for you to find a job? I don't imagine that there were many PR jobs floating around at that time."

"True. Jobs were scarce when I graduated. There were one or two positions available on the West coast in the L.A. area but we didn't want to move there."

"I can empathize with that."

"Should have turned gambler at that time. Lady luck took a liking to me. I landed an interesting job in Naval Archives as a researcher. It didn't pay what I would have liked but it was putting bread on the table."

"I was never much of a gambler either. Did your luck continue?"

"Did it ever. My boss liked me. He had a close friend, in the form of Senator Martin who was the chairman of the Senate Armed

Services Committee. I was introduced to the senator at a cocktail party. I found that he was looking for an Administrative Assistant. He expressed an interest in my background and PR degree."

"You got the job?"

"Yes, sir, I did, and after several long interviews he chose me over twelve others. Neat, huh?"

"Congratulations again, Paul. That was a real kudos for you."

"Thank you, sir."

Paul and I chatted for a bit, but the high noise level was starting to bother both of us. We decided to go up to my room. We spent the better part of two hours and a couple of Scotches filling each other in on what had happened in our lives. Then the phone rang. It was Carl reminding me that he had signed us up for the sub base tour the next morning. I thanked him and got back to Burgess. In a short while, I suggested that Paul and I go out to dinner at a restaurant where Don Ho was performing. On our way out we passed the convention desk where Paul also signed up for the sub base tour the next day.

As we entered the restaurant, Polynesian music and the aroma of Frangipani and Plumeria enveloped us. The dark and colorful tropical vegetation with ample giant bamboo in the background looked authentic. The sound of a heavy tropical rain filled the air periodically. The usual sign "Please wait to be seated" was , of course, prominent. As the Chinese hostess approached us out of the dimly lit interior, I gasped. She was wearing a shimmering, iridescent, turquoise Cheongsam; a close fitting dress with a high necked Mandarin collar with two slits part way up the sides. Chinese women traditionally wear them for dressy or formal occasions. With her raven hair in a swept up style, she was strikingly beautiful. Having heard my gasp, Paul asked:

"Captain, do you know her?"

"No, Paul, she just reminded me of some one I once knew."

After selecting a table and starting to order I said hello to the waitress in Cantonese. She responded appropriately and we exchanged a few words.

Paul was taken aback by this and asked, "Can you speak

Chinese?"

"Only a small bit of Cantonese and not very well at that."

The menu had a wide variety of choices so we took sometime selecting. We enjoyed our leisurely dinner while some soft Hawaiian music played in the background. During the meal we shared more experiences. When we finished we strolled back to the Royal and went to my room for a night cap. The message light on my telephone was flashing. It was a call from Carl saying that he wanted to meet me for breakfast in the morning. I called his room. He wasn't in but I left a message saying I'd meet him in a restaurant down the street. Braun and I had developed a long lasting friendship from our time on the *Blackfin*.

I filled Paul in on my relationship with Carl. I told him how I had rescued Carl from the clutches of the Shore Patrol in San Diego one night and how he in turn saved my fanny by not saying anything about an engine problem to the Captain. He had taken care of the problem very quickly and very quietly. Nobody was the wiser. I was striving to be the best submarine officer I could be and, as a Naval Reservist, I would not have looked very good in the Captain's eyes. I had to keep my best foot forward at all times.

Paul told me about some of the inner workings of the Senator's office including a glimpse into the power that his boss, as well as all the other senators, wielded in the process of governing. It sounded like a high powered position and I was glad to see how well he seemed to be able to cope with the pressures of his job. I could appreciate what he was saying since I once had a tour of duty in the Office of Legislative Affairs for the Navy out of the Pentagon. Navy liaison to the Senate and Senate liaison to the Navy. That tour was full of pressure but very interesting and eye opening. But above all, Paul seemed to have retained a fine family relationship. I envied him and went to sleep that night with a sense that all was right in this world.

At breakfast Carl was exuberant. He had lined up three different phases of the sub base tour that he figured that I'd like. I told him I had invited Paul Burgess to join us and that didn't seem to bother him. In fact he seem to be delighted to be in the company of two officers and took charge of our tour. Carl's enthusiasm insured we were among the first to board the bus. Carl had brought a friend of his along so that he would also have a seat companion. I thought that was very astute of him. This allowed me to do some more chatting with Burgess during the ride.

As the bus started to unload at the submarine base, I was startled by a shape rising from one of the front rows. He was wearing one of those vests that identified him as a World War II submariner. Unmistakably, the flat top haircut on a round head atop a plump body could have belonged to nobody else but "Porky" from my days on the *Dolphin*.

Startled, I yelled, "Hey, Porky! Wait up."

When the man turned to see who was calling I knew for sure it was Porky. He looked back at me with a dull stare. He showed no signs of recognition or emotion. No smile. No frown. Instead he seemed to turn pale and hurried off the bus. There was no way I could push my way through the crowd of ex-submariners all trying to get off the bus at once. Keyed up at the thought of meeting an old shipmate with whom I shared some memorable experiences, I got off the bus and looked around, but he was nowhere in sight. A fellow tourist nudged me.

"That guy you wanted to see? He just got in that taxi over there."

"Thanks."

I saw the taxi leave, heading for the main gate. What was going on? We had a good relationship on the *Dolphin*. A cold shudder passed through my body. I couldn't figure out why I felt that way. For a second I thought back to the days aboard the *Dolphin*.

Paul put his arm on my shoulder.

"Captain, What was that all about? You seemed to know him and the way he left he obviously wanted to avoid you. He apparently ran away. Could you possibly have been mistaken?"

"I wasn't mistaken, Paul. I have a good memory for both names and faces. It was Porky, all right."

"Why wouldn't he enjoy seeing you again?"

"I don't know, Paul. That bothers me."

We walked over toward the diving tower along with the group. Almost every submarine sailor who passed through Pearl Harbor had practiced sunken submarine escapes in that tank, learning to use the famous "Momsen Lung." As a young Quartermaster, many years ago, I spent hours on top of that structure practicing blinker code with a signal light to other stations and ships in the region. Some of the group decided to climb the stairs that circled up around the out side of the 110 foot high tower where they could get an overall view of the base as well as all of Pearl Harbor. Paul and I decided that that was too much of an exercise for two old salts and sat down on a nearby bench.

Another bus with a group from the hotel pulled up next to ours. We casually watched the guys getting off the bus and setting foot on the Sub Base for the first time in maybe 60 years. I couldn't believe my eyes when I recognized a tall, thin grey haired man, also wearing one of those blue vests, step down off the bus. It was none other than "Ding-Dong" Bell, one of the Quartermaster gang on *Dolphin*. He still had those large freckles that he had when I knew him from before. I got up off the bench and headed toward him. He appeared to be joking with some men as I approached, but when he saw me, his smile vanished.

"Ding-Dong, don't you remember me? Swede! We were in the Quartermaster gang aboard the *Dolphin*."

"Ah! ...I'm sorry. You caught me by surprise...er...ah...Swede, I'm with the guys from my boat; the *Swordfish*. I,...ah,... I, ... I'm sorry but we have a tight schedule and I'll try to get back to you later."

His stammering and lack of smile showed me he was shaken up at seeing me again. Ding-Dong hurried off with his fellow *Swordfish* shipmates. He looked as if he had just awakened from a bad dream. He didn't ask me where I was staying. Could he have just assumed I was staying at the Royal? Paul, who was at my right, spoke up again.

"Captain! What the hell's going on? That guy got all shook up when he saw you. The guy on the bus left in a hurry. Something is not right here. Can you shed some light on this? What about the

Dolphin? Apparently you were aboard her. Is that right?"

Deep in thought, I had momentarily gone back again to the days on *Dolphin* when I last saw Ding-dong. Paul persisted:

"Captain! Where are you?"

"Sorry Paul. Just give me a minute. I was thinking about something."

I drifted back again. I hadn't seen or thought about those two guys for over sixty years. Maybe they had forgotten the trials we went through together before the attack on Pearl Harbor. He referred to the *Swordfish* as his boat. What about the *Dolphin*? Perhaps they had remembered a warning we had received about …? Suddenly there was a loud whack nearby. Startled, I looked in the direction of the noise. A coconut had fallen off one of the palm trees that were scattered around the base. Back in reality, I had a sinking feeling in the pit of my stomach.

"This is not the place to talk about this, Paul. I have to get back to the Royal ASAP."

"I'll go with you. You seem pretty upset."

"If you'd like, Paul, but I won't be good company."

"Well, sir, I think you need some company anyway so I'll just tag along if you don't mind."

"Be my guest."

I beckoned to Carl and when he came over, I told him that I had to get back to the hotel, and maybe we could finish the tour the next day. He looked puzzled but he nodded that he understood. Paul and I grabbed a taxi and headed back. At the hotel I went up to the convention headquarters with Paul close behind me. The area was almost deserted, with all the tours going on and happy hour in the hospitality room was still quite a few hours away. I headed toward the alcove that contained the "Boat Books."

The "Boat Books" were binders labeled A - C, D - G and so forth. I grabbed the D - G binder and thumbed through it until I came to the *Dolphin*. There were signatures indicating that some *Dolphin* sailors had checked in, but I knew that most of them had been aboard before or after the time when we were in so much trouble. None of the sailors names on the list had been aboard *Dolphin* between October 1 until December 7, 1941. I double checked to see whether there was another page for *Dolphin* under V-7, D-1, or SS-169; other possible designations for the *Dolphin*. There were no other pages. Yet, I had seen two *Dolphin* sailors from that harrowing time the three of us were aboard her. Why hadn't Porky and Ding-Dong signed in? Carl indicated, it was customary to do so. Absorbed in thought, I had forgotten that Paul had accompanied me to the boat books alcove, and, when I turned I bumped right smack into him.

"Sorry, Paul. My mind was somewhere else."

"That was obvious, sir. What's the scoop?"

"Let's go down to the outside bar for a Mai Tai. We can have a little privacy and wont be interrupted. I hope that little place is still there."

"Suits me, Captain."

We found the little hideaway lounge that I knew from the time when I was assigned as C.O. of the *Sabalo*. My Division Commander had introduced it to me. The bar was situated so you could look out over the beach. It was shaded by palm trees. It had a pretty good view of Diamond Head. We gazed off at tourists riding an out-rigger canoe atop the waves entering the bay. There seemed to be hundreds of dots along the shore line in the waves - people body surfing.

"This is nice isn't it, Paul?"

"It sure is. I would never have spotted this place."

We ordered a couple of Mai Tais and sat down at the slightly rusting table. The salt water had done a number on the metal chairs. Paul fidgeted and stared at me as if to say, "I'm waiting for more."

I wondered if I was doing the right thing even broaching the fact that I had ever served aboard *Dolphin*. But I had already let the cat out of the bag. On an impulse, I started to tell Paul my story. If I hadn't quit smoking many years earlier, I would have lit up then for sure.

"I was a quartermaster on the *Dolphin* for a number of years and had many good experiences aboard her at the Canal Zone, in operations in and out of San Diego, and here in Pearl Harbor in late 1941."

"That must have been five or six years?"

"It was, and I enjoyed most of that time in spite of the fact that the *Dolphin* was so old. Even so, it was a hell of lot better than the O boats I trained on at New London. Anyway, as you noticed, I bumped into a couple of old shipmates from the *Dolphin* out at the base, Porky and Ding-Dong, and they acted mighty strange."

"That sure got my attention, Captain. What's behind it?"

"Just now you saw me check the boat books."

"Yes, sir."

"Porky and Ding-dong were both on *Dolphin* at that time but they haven't signed in. Nor has anyone else who was on there during that time. Others who were aboard her before and during the war have signed in. Why hasn't anybody else signed in? In particular, Porky and Ding-Dong. While I wasn't looking for it, I didn't notice any *Dolphin* name on their vests when I saw them out at the base today."

"What period of time are you talking about, Captain?"

"Late 1941."

"Before we got into World War II?"

"That's right. Six months to a year or so before."

"That was a relatively calm period for the Navy, wasn't it?"

"Yes, sort of. But that wasn't a universal situation. I remember that some of the low level of activity was due to orders from the top to conserve on Bunker-C fuel oil. That meant that the Carriers, Battle ships, and Cruisers stayed in port a lot of the time. As far as submarines were concerned that didn't seem to be a problem. A lot of the newer boats of the Porpoise, Salmon, and Tambor classes' seemed to be flushing into and out of Pearl. They would operate out of here for awhile and then the be shuttled off to the Asiatic Fleet in the Phillippines. Actually there were some aspects that gave our situation a slightly different slant. Several of the submarines, including *Dolphin*, based at Pearl had been performing simulated war patrols around Midway and Wake. They were mostly two to three weeks duration. We were supposed to get acquainted with war time conditions or what the Navy thought, then, those conditions might be like. This problem is bothering me. I 've got to think about this a little bit. It may be more serious than I thought. I'm going up to my room, Paul."

"Mind if I tag along?"

"I don't mind, if you think you can stand being with me while I try to figure out this enigma."

Up in my room, I poured a couple of scotches and kicked my shoes off. Paul sat on the ratan lounging chair which allowed him to look out the window and see me at the same time. I paced back and forth for a few moments. I stopped and turned to face Paul.

"Captain, what's bothering you? Do you want to tell me?"

"I'm thinking about something that I've kept bottled up for a long time, Paul. I need to tell someone my story. It might as well be you. I have to get it off my chest sometime before I die."

"I'm all ears, Captain."

"Paul, just like you, most people who know me think they know my story. From enlisted rating, E-1 to commissioned rank, O-6, right?"

"You're a true Mustang, Captain. You really made it the hard way being enlisted before being commissioned. You can be proud of that."

"Haven't you spotted a gap in my career, Paul?"

"No sir, I haven't. There was no gap that I was aware of."

"As you may remember, I received a commission as an Ensign in the Naval Reserve at the end of the World War II. The first distinction that I achieved was to become the oldest Ensign in the Navy, Regular or Reserve. I lacked self confidence in those days. As a commissioned officer I gained some much needed self esteem under guidance of some fine Naval Academy officers I served under. I became more confident. When I grew more senior and more professional as a submarine officer I had the audacity to aspire to Flag rank. But that wasn't to be, and the experience I had on the *Dolphin* just before the war could have been the reason for my not being selected for Rear Admiral. I know I will never find out what occurred behind the closed doors of the Selection Board, but whatever happened precluded my ever reaching flag rank. Age then kept my records from appearing before another board."

"Have you any idea what might have kept you from being selected? Could it have been something that you did or said?"

"That is something that I have kept silent about for more than 60 years, but the story needs to get out. Paul, it looks like you're the one to whom I should tell my story."

"Go ahead, Captain. How can I help?"

"Remember, I said something appeared to be missing from my record–a gap that no one notices or dares to ask about. I want to tell you what happened, Paul. Maybe I'm taking a chance on talking about it now, but at my age what's the difference?"

"What're you saying, Captain?"

"My health is good and I have no desire to leave this world at any time soon. The Freedom of Information Act doesn't yet allow this story to be told. I don't know why an event that happened over sixty years ago should still be classified as Top Secret but it is. The bureaucracy and the media would have a field day with this if it ever got out."

"You mean the government might take some action against you?"

"Put it this way, Paul. I'm worried. A few years ago newspaper articles told of the death of a Cabinet Secretary who had become an embarrassment to the President politically. He died in a C-130 crash in Turkey if I remember correctly. It occurred in broad day-light and clear weather. Another story covered the CIA giving the green light to the assassination of two American citizens in Chile who were supporting a regime that our President was opposed to. An old shipmate of mine from the *Dolphin*, Clyde Smith, died recently under very peculiar circumstances. His wife, Elaine, called and asked me if I could find out what had happened to him. She was only told that he died of natural causes. I couldn't find out anything. Every avenue I explored turned out to be a blind alley. I began to wonder. Clyde, was a world class, marathon talker. Yak, yak, yak all the time. The thought occurred to me that his penchant for gab possibly included some bits about our prewar experiences aboard the *Dolphin* and may have led to his untimely death. A number of that crew have been reported as having passed away, some sooner than later, if you know what I mean."

"Are you saying the CIA might have killed your shipmate and might try to bump you off if you let this story out?"

"Could be, Paul. But it would more likely be the NSA rather than the CIA."

"The NSA ?"

"The National Security Agency."

"How do they fit in?"

"You don't hear much about them. They're the **real** "Black Helicopter" people. They have twice the staff and twice the budget of the CIA. Ask your boss about them sometime. Maybe even he doesn't know much about them."

"Do you trust me enough to tell me what happened? If there's any problem, I'm sure I can get Senator Martin to go to bat for you. Together we pack a lot of influence with the Navy up on the Hill."

"Forget about the Senator, Paul, I don't want anybody other than you to hear my story."

"Yes sir."

"I've got no choice, Paul. I trust you. I have to tell this to someone before... Well, before I tell you my story I want you to swear to God that you wont tell anyone while I'm alive. OK?"

"Sure, but I don't think it's necessary."

"Maybe, but what I'm about to tell you is still Top Secret. I don't know what kind of a clearance you have. I'm taking a chance revealing this even if you were to have the required clearance because you don't have the 'need to know.'"

"Even at this late date?"

"Yes. Even at this late date. However, I have a stronger need to tell this story than to bury it and start worrying again."

I got the Gideon Bible out of the night stand made Paul put his hand on it and swear not to divulge anything that I was about to tell him to anybody. Ever!

Chapter II: In the Beginning

This is my story with all the details I can remember from 60 or so years ago. They are as vivid to me today as though it was yesterday. I have never written any of this down for fear it could fall into the wrong hands. I believed it could spell trouble for me, even now. I've been tempted to write it all down and put it in my safety deposit box, but I knew they could even get into that. So here goes.

In late 1941 the United States Navy's Pacific Fleet needed intelligence about Japanese Naval operations. This information, it turned out, would have been critical. They needed a way find out what the Japanese Navy was doing. Their obvious best choice was a submarine. It could get where they needed it without detection. They chose the *Dolphin* to perform this task. The *Dolphin* had the range to get to Japanese waters and back. I first knew her as the *D-1* when I reported aboard at Coco Solo in the Panama Canal Zone. Her hull number was 169. At that time she was officially referred to as a "cruiser type" submarine.

Some of the Motor Machinist mates aboard called her the *Dirty D* because she had so many hydraulic oil leaks and her engines seemed to bleed oil. Her riveted construction spawned diesel oil leaks from the fuel and fuel-oil ballast tanks. Moreover, we were accused of being the only submarine in the Navy with a million dollar conning tower/bridge. It seems that the conning tower fair-water had been fabricated out of Corrosion Resisting Steel (CRS). Someone in the Bureau of Ships, called the Bureau of Construction and Repair in those days, got the idea that the CRS would cut down on the salt water corrosion of the superstructure which was a universal problem in the submarine force. The Navy experimented with the *Dolphin*. The crew got kidded a lot about that. No other submarine had that kind of bridge structure at the time and to put one on such an old boat everyone thought was stupid. She made a good, cheap test platform.

Some old timers may remember a movie released in 1937 called, *Submarine D-1*, that featured the old *Dolphin*. The movie starred Pat O'Brian, George Brent, Wayne Morris, Frank McHugh and Broderick Crawford. I shook hands with several of these actors. Incidentally, former President Ronald Reagan was originally in it as well but he ended up on the cutting room floor. I was not able to meet him or see him at the time. As I recall it was a class B movie. The movie portrayed the sinking of the *Squalus* and the loss of life as well as the rescue of many of the men aboard. It demonstrated the use of the new McCann Rescue Chamber (diving bell) and Momsen Lung in a dramatic manner.

As it turned out the *Dolphin* became the prototype of the fleet submarine that became so famous during World War II, fully capable of making independent extended patrols. The *Dolphin* had six torpedo tubes. Four forward and two aft. She had the ability to travel approximately 15,000 miles or more without refueling. This fact was to be a major plus for our submarines because it enabled us, later, to bring the war to the home waters of the Empire of Japan. At the time the Navy had no idea that submarines would play such an important role in the ensuing war with Japan. *Dolphin* was in Submarine Division 42 of Squadron Four, at Pearl Harbor, and considered part of the Navy's Scouting force. The battleship admirals in those days considered submarines a necessary evil. Battleships were called dreadnaughts and were considered unsinkable. The admirals believed that submarines were good only for scouting.

Once they discovered the location of the enemy they were to report the contact to the battle fleet and then harass any stragglers. There were one or two of the top brass that figured that submarines could stalk enemy warships in their home waters and provide information of value to the battle fleet. When one of the senior battleship admirals suggested that submarines could get realistic training by being used to scout the waters of the Imperial Japanese Empire, other admirals promptly vetoed the suggestion as being too provocative considering the tense international situation that existed at the time. The United Sates had stopped shipping scrap iron and oil to Japan and was warning Japan not to expand in to southeast Asia.

    I was a Quartermaster First Class aboard the *Dolphin*. My shipmate and long time good friend, Clyde Hammer, was an Engineman. We called them Motor Machinist Mates in those days. Clyde, was an Auxilliaryman. He performed most of his duties in the control room and in the pump room just below the control room. I performed mine in the conning tower and on the bridge. Clyde and Harry Sullivan (Sully), a Machinist Mate, were running mates and often went ashore on liberty together. Harry spent his time in the engine room. I was pretty much of a loner. On occasion Clyde and Sully would invite me to go on liberty with them. Personally, I enjoyed reading, swimming at Waikiki beach, sight seeing and visiting museums. A live concert would have been very satisfactory for me, though it was not my shipmate's cup of tea. I was not married at the time and very few of my shipmates were.

    I had adapted to submarine life very well. Perhaps it was the fact that as a child, my mother could not get me to take a nap which I do almost every day now. Back then I could not go to sleep while the sun was up. On a submarine, when it is submerged you don't seem to be conscious of whether the sun is up or not, so I slept soundly any time of day. Surfaced or submerged. I easily tuned myself into the internal rhythms of the ship and seemed to sense when a change in noise level merely meant that an engine was coming on line or going off line or was an emergency. I was mentally prepared to program my mind to the events that were scheduled to occur. I was aware of battery charges and trim dives. An unscheduled drill would cause me to wake up momentarily and as soon as I recognized it was a drill and didn't require my presence I would go right back to sleep.

    The first Friday morning in port after three weeks at sea on a simulated war patrol off Midway Island, Clyde looked up over his cup of coffee as I paused to draw my own cup in Crew's Mess.

"Hey, Swede. How'd you like to hit the beach with me and Sully today? Want to take in some rays with us?"

They wanted to spend time basking in the sun at Waikiki. All of us needed or wanted to overcome the ghostly pallor that most submariners had. You could almost always spot a submarine sailor in Honolulu by his pale complexion. Your military garb always had a faint odor of diesel oil and you didn't have to look too hard to detect small holes in the clothing. These holes were caused by traces of electrolyte from the batteries picked up and distributed by the ships ventilation system.

"Sounds good to me, Clyde. I got to go pick up some charts and a couple of new binoculars for the Captain and Exec. Can I join you later?"

"See you in front of Fort DeRussy about 1200, OK?"

"I'll do my best to be there on time."

A little late getting off to go on liberty, I managed to grab the 1000 bus to Honolulu, but the Dole Company's *Pineapple Express* train held us up for nearly twenty-five minutes. The train passed the sub base just outside the Makalapa gate twice a day. A small narrow gauge steam engine with its gondola cars loaded with freshly cut pineapple took its time to go by. I'll always remember the acid-sweet aroma of the freshly harvested fruit as it passed by en route to the Dole cannery near the Matson Steamship Line pier. The cannery could be easily found. It had a large water tower in the shape of a huge pineapple.

On the way into Honolulu the bus passed the Hawaiian Territorial prison. In each direction someone had placed large crudely lettered signs that read "Caution: Prisoners Escaping." The frequent escapes from this prison made headlines in the Honolulu Star-Bulletin almost weekly. Security was poor. Remember, Hawaii was a territory of the United States in those days, not a state. All our U.S. money had an over print that stated "Territory of the United States."

In those days Oahu, and in particular, Honolulu, had a particular kind of casual rural charm that seemed to permeate new comers insidiously. The guys called it Polynesian Paralysis. While meandering along Beretania or Hotel streets someone would bump into you, offer an apology, and hurry on by. That was a sure way to identify a newcomer to the island. Polynesian Paralysis hadn't set in yet. Another thing that I remember were the school type busses with only a front entrance. They didn't have rear exits. They were not well kept and the salt air had worked its corrosive ability on them. They smoked and belched oily noxious exhaust fumes when ever they stopped to pick up passengers. The taxis were better and most of us used them when we could. If four or five of us got a cab the fare was only slightly more than the bus. Now and then, a modern bus would appear and we learned that Honolulu was fast becoming modernized.

Delaying my trip to the beach, I decided to get my hair cut at Gloria's. Gloria was a Chinese girl who cut peoples hair. Her barber shop was a stool on the side walk in front of a place on Hotel Street. She cut my hair regularly. I watched her while she finished cutting an Oriental man's hair. She pocketed the man's money in the sash-like purse she had strapped around her waist and swept the cuttings into a long handled dust pan. She looked pretty with her bangs and straight black hair. It was a hair style typical of most of the Chinese women then in Hawaii. Her tight fitting black trousers showed her figure off to good advantage. Her slipper like black shoes made her feet look small. She glanced up with her almond eyes and saw me. The look on her face changed immediately from impassive to surprised. She gave me a quick affectionate hug. We chatted as she cut my hair and she told all the little things that she had been doing while I was out at sea. She hugged me again. As a prelude to a kiss, she gently rubbed her little nose against mine.

"Are you sure you are not an Eskimo? I told you that's the way Eskimos kiss not Caucasians. Do it right please." She giggled like a little girl.

I have always been partial to oriental girls and I thought Gloria was pretty. She had a warm personality and I liked her. Her Chinese name was Meilin which I thought had a nice sound to it and I called her by it all the time. It means "Beautiful Jade" in Cantonese. After a few haircuts, we became friends and started dating. She invited me to join her family for the Chinese New Year's celebration each year for two of the three years that *Dolphin* had been home ported at Pearl. I was looking forward to the next gathering at her family's house.

Meilin's family spoke little English. They were a nice, friendly family. Her father, a rather thin and small man worked as a cook at the Naval Shipyard cafeteria and her mother, a round faced, cheerful lady who worked part time at a near by restaurant. Meilin had two sisters, both married, one to a Caucasian, and the other married to a Chinese man and they had three of the cutest little children. Her brother was also married to a Chinese lady and they had four children. I enjoyed the family immensely, especially her nieces and nephews. I learned to speak a little Cantonese from the kids.

At that time I didn't know much about Chinese customs. I have since found out that the ritual Chinese New Year's dinner which consisted of duck, pork, chicken and tofu topped off by a whole fish, delightfully poached, is served in a precise order. The fish is served last and the head of the fish, when placed on the table, is always pointed in the direction of the guest of honor. I was pleased when I found it always pointed toward me.

Meilin and I shared the same feelings about many things. On many a liberty, after basking on the beach or sight seeing, I would spend the evening with Meilin at her apartment listening to records like, "In the Mood,""Tuxedo Junction," or "Green Eyes." She liked Swing just as much as I did. One night I took her to see the just released cartoon movie, *Fantasia,* by Walt Disney. She went bananas over that and really enjoyed it. It gave me an opportunity to introduce her to some of my favorite classical music. Sometimes we'd go out to dinner. One evening I was curious because she persuaded me to take her to the Wu Fat restaurant and cabaret. She said she had a surprise for me. The surprise was that the owner of the restaurant, on the second floor, was a relative of hers. I believe he was her uncle. There was a bar at street level that several of the *Dolphin* sailors used to enjoy from time to time.

Whenever Meilin and I went to that or any other restaurant, I was proud to be seen with her. She looked terrific in one of those slim dresses with those tantalizing slits up the side. She wore that type of dress whenever we went to a dress up affair. One evening after going out to dinner as I said good bye she put her arms around me and I summoned up the courage to kiss her. As her face and mind grew close she raised up on her tiptoes and rubbed her nose against mine. I kissed her and reminded her about the Eskimo tradition of affection. She laughed. She became a good, sincere friend. Haircut finished I walked over to the Y.

At the Y.M.C.A. on Beretania street, I changed into my civies and carefully folded up my white uniform and put it in the locker I had rented. The Y was cheaper than the Locker Clubs and I thought better, too. It also had a swimming pool which I would use occasionally. I decided to get a bite at the Black Cat Café across the street from the Y before heading for Fort DeRussy. It was popular with all the servicemen in Honolulu. You could get a complete breakfast of bacon and eggs with a glass of papaya juice and toast for 45 cents. Their wonderful Kona coffee was free. A cheese burger cost twenty cents. Most of the submariners liked Oyster stew or hamburgers. I still have a menu, in a frame at home, that I took from the Black Cat.

I caught up with Clyde and Sully at Fort De Russy about 12:15. Heavy set Sully with his sparse strands of black hair waving in the zephyr-like breeze was sitting on a nearby bench spoke to me.

"Swede, what kept you?"

"I needed a haircut so I stopped at Gloria's."

"You still seeing that Chink?"

"Knock it off, Sully. She's a damn nice girl and I don't like your calling her Chink"

"OK, OK, I'm sorry, Swede. Didn't know you were serious about her. You thinking of getting hitched?"

"Sully, it's none of your damn business, but I could do a lot worse."

"I won't say another word."

"Fine. Don't say anything. You should never use the word 'Chink.'"

TOP SECRET

Black Cat Café
Honolulu, Hawaii

Breakfast Dishes

Hot Cakes.................$	.10
Waffle...................	.15
Oatmeal..................	.15
Corn Flakes..............	.15
Ham, Bacon or Sausage & eggs Buttered Toast and hash Browns...................	.35
Poached eggs on toast.....	.30
Egg & tomato scramble.....	.30
Oyster omelette...........	.45
Hard boiled egg, pickled egg, or raw egg...............	.05

24-Hour Specials

Breaded Veal cutlet.......	.35
Roast Turkey with dressing	.50
½ Fried Chicken with bacon	.60
Roast Pork & applesauce...	.40
Swiss Steak & brown gravy.	.25
Corned Beef & Cabbage.....	.30
Spaghetti & Meatballs.....	.25
Hot Pork or Beef sandwich.	.25

Steaks, Chops and other meats

Porterhouse & mushrooms..	1.25
T-Bone....................	.60
Rib Eye steak.............	.40
Hamburger .30, with onions	.35
Liver & onions .30 w/bacon	.35

Fish & Sea Foods

½ doz. Fresh Frozen Oysters fried, stewed, or raw....	.35
Fried Shrimps on toast....	.35
Fried Ulua, tarter sauce..	.30

Salads

Fruit salad with whipped cream............	.25
Crab......................	.50
Shrimp....................	.35
Potato....................	.15
Aligator Pear.............	.10

Cold Meats

Boiled Ham...............$	.35
Assorted Cold cuts........	.35
Pig's feet................	.20
Sardines..................	.25

Soups

Chicken...................	.20
Corn Chowder..............	.20
Vegetable.................	.20
Turtle....................	.20

Sandwiches

(Any sandwich under .20 - on Toast .05 extra) Potato salad with any sandwich .10

Black Cat Special.........	.20
Bacon & Egg...............	.20
Cold ham..................	.10
Bacon & Tomato............	.20
Hamburger.................	.15
Hamburger & cheese........	.20
Peanut butter.............	.10
Club House................	.50
Denver....................	.25
Barbequed Beef............	.15
Hot dog...................	.10

Desserts

Strawberry shortcake with Whipped cream............	.20
Pies (per cut)............	.10
Pie a la mode.............	.15
Brown bobbies.......2 for	.05
Ice Cream.................	.10
Banana Split..............	.25

Drinks

Buttermilk................	.10
Milk (second glass .05)..	.10
Postum....................	.10
Ovaltine..................	.10
Milk Shakes...............	.15
Malted Milks..............	.20
Coca Cola & other sodas..	.10
with meals...............	.05

The three of us headed over to Waikiki beach. We changed into our swimming trunks and headed down to the beach, which turned out to be virtually deserted that day. Glancing over the sparse crowd we could see that it was composed predominately of males and most of them, I'm sure, were soldiers or sailors on liberty.

"Where are all the dames today?" grumbled Sully.

"Clyde calls the girls 'broads'. How come you're different?"

"Swede, when you get as old as Clyde and me you'll call them all kinds of different names."

"Not me. You guys don't have any respect for ladies. I have a lot of respect for the gentler sex."

"Swede! Grow up. Women are clever creatures."

"Seriously, I think the main reason for the lack of females is that the Lurline probably hasn't docked yet this week."

"You may be right there, Swede."

Glancing over the sparse crowd we could see they appeared to be mostly men. They were probably soldiers or sailors. The Matson Liners, the Lurline or the Matsonia, usually docked every seven or eight days. That was likely the reason we didn't have much in the way of pretty wahinis lying on the beach. Some of us used to go down to the harbor in Honolulu by the Aloha Tower from time to time and watch the passengers disembarking from the Matson line ships. We always hoped we would see some of the animated, giggling girls on the beach in their one piece bathing suits. Bikinis hadn't been invented yet. Most of the young girls had either parents or chaperones who slowly followed their animated charges who were to be seen bouncing down the gangway.

Pan American's China Clipper air service from the mainland had its base at Pearl City on the peninsula opposite the Middle Loch of Pearl Harbor. Honolulu was its first stop on their island hoping way to Singapore. Pan Am bussed their, mostly male, passengers to and from the Royal Hawaiian hotel for an overnight stay. That did not, however, contribute much to the feminine population on the beach.

"Hey! Wow! Look at that," Sully muttered as a lone female passed about ten yards away.

She was so covered with a tatami mat, towels and a large, floppy hat that you could scarcely tell it was a female. I looked over at Sully and thought that he needed more time ashore when a bunch of towels could excite him.

"It doesn't take much to get you excited, Sully. Maybe you should visit the Hurricane deck."

Lying on the warm sand we thought some more about the female tourists in their swimming suits. The warm, gentle trade winds seemed to embrace us as we talked. We started discussing the *Dolphin's* much needed overhaul and talking helped submerge our hormonal urges.

"I sure hope we get some time in the Navy Yard soon. I can't overhaul our air compressors aboard ship any more and a three week up-keep won't begin to solve that problem," Clyde said. "I'm tired of trying to fix 'em up with chewing gum and baling wire."

"You think you got problems with your goddamn air compressors?" Sully added, "You ought to be back in the engine room with me. Them engines are always wiping out bearings and we need to take the engines apart and install new bearings, which have to be blued, scraped and fitted first and then reinstalled again. Even then we sometimes have to take the engines apart again and repeat the process until we get the right fit. I hope we get new engines at the Navy yard. The old ones are a bitch to live with what with their breaking down all the time. They just can't seem to take running at full power for any length of time."

"I'd like to see us get one of those new Torpedo Data Computers that I heard about. I have to do too much figuring when we make a torpedo firing approach. Besides it's so crowded in our tiny conning tower that it's difficult to get any calculating done."

"We couldn't hit the broadside of a barn firing torpedoes from 125 feet deep even if we had a computer. Why don't we just fire a random spread in the general direction of the target and hope and pray to get a hit," snorted Clyde.

"No," I argued. "We get pretty good dope from sonar and if we used the Is-Was we could come pretty close."

"What the hell is the Is-Was?"

"The Is-Was is a type of circular slide rule made out of that new plastic stuff. You set it up based on the last periscope observation of the target and it also shows the previous observation. From that you could project fairly accurately where the target was likely to be. The Captain always asked: 'Where *is* the target now?' Hence *is-was*. I just wish we could verify the dope with a periscope observation now and then."

With a newer device called the "Banjo" because it was shaped like one, that showed both our position as well as the target's, we could get pretty good firing information. Skippers in those days almost always made sonar approaches but Middle of Target hits (MOT's) were very scarce. Periscope observations were considered to be too easily spotted from the air to be safe. We didn't have the thin battle scopes that our submarines had later on in World War II. The top brass also figured that a submarine or its shadow could also be seen from the air, so sonar approaches became the norm.

Clyde groaned as he picked up his straw hat and covered up his bald spot again. His sunken cheeks and hollow looking eye sockets peering out from under the shadow of that hat made him look like a cadaver.

Sully asked, "Swede, do you know anything about the new sonar they installed the last time we were in dry dock?"

"Not much, But I think that it's a combination of the old one that uses crystals and the new one that uses metal rods and cones and sends out pings and echo ranges like a destroyer. It's called the JK-QC. The JK has the crystals and the QC has the rods and cones."

"What does that mean?"

"I don't know much about it but as far as I know the first sonar on our submarines had crystals called Piezoelectric crystals. The crystals were made from Rochelle salt. They could receive sound under water extremely well. They weren't able to send signals however. We needed to be able to send signals to get an echo in order to determine an accurate range to the target and maybe also communicate with our surface escorts. The QC part, which could send signals as well as hear sounds and receive the generated echos was added to the head. One side was JK and the other was QC. You had to turn the head 180 degrees to switch from one to the other."

"Don't our destroyers send out pings when they're looking for subs?"

"Yeah. They've been doing that for some time. Nobody ever thought that submarines would ever need to do that too. Destroyers never had a JK sonar that I know of; only a QC type."

"That's too much for my weak brain to think about."

I noticed that Sully was getting sunburned. His nose and belly were red. I had just told him he should turn over when we heard a voice with a strong mid-western accent calling for any *Dolphin* sailors to make themselves known. The voice sounded familiar. Looking up we saw Ding-Dong Bell, our Second Class Quartermaster aboard the *Dolphin*. He was a tall, lanky, and sandy-haired man with prominent red freckles. As he walked along the beach wearing a Shore Patrol arm band, the Blue dolphins on the sleeve of his white jumper indicated he was qualified in submarines. We yelled at Ding-Dong and waved. He hurried over. " Y o u guys got to get back to the boat right away."

I suddenly had a chilling feeling as if a large dark cloud was passing between me and the sun.

"How come?" Sully asked.

"I think we're going to be getting underway soon. There's somepin' big goin' on."

That cloud shadow got darker and I felt the chill deepen. I couldn't explain that feeling even if my life were to depend on it.

"When I left the boat this morning I thought we were supposed to have at least a two week up-keep starting Monday," I grumbled.

I had firmly believed that we weren't going to get underway for at least another two weeks or hopefully, three weeks. Someone had passed on some scuttlebutt that this time we would get an interim docking at the Navy Yard and would be in port for about a month. There were all kinds of repairs needed throughout the boat which I personally believed should have had a very high priority.

"Do you know where any of the other guys are?" Ding-Dong asked.

"Chief Brown and a couple of guys from the forward room said they were on their way to the Monkey Bar at the Pearl City Tavern for a couple of drinks when I left the boat," I volunteered.

"Your buddy, Ding-a-Ling has the duty so you won't have to search for him."

There were two sailors aboard named Bell and since we usually called each other by our last names, we provided each of them with appropriate nick-names. Another sailor we dubbed "Mattress Back" because it seemed that he hardly ever got out of the rack. Nicknames were standard. Rhodes became "Dusty," Lanes became "Shady" and so forth. An Electrician friend of mine was dubbed "Shakey" from the way he jumped when someone snapped a pencil behind his neck. My nickname was "Swede" because of my Swedish ancestry. The officers always called us by our last names mostly to avoid becoming too familiar with the enlisted men. There was a saying among them that "Familiarity Breeds Contempt" and we couldn't have contempt for our officers. We gathered up our things and headed back.

Clyde spoke up. "I guess that cancels the soft ball game with the *Narwhal* tomorrow. I was hoping we'd get even for that trouncing they gave us last month. Besides, I like the San Miguel beer they provided."

"I didn't want to play tomorrow anyway. My knee is bothering me again."

"Sully, you're always complaining about something. What'll it be next time?"

The submarines operating regularly out of Pearl had an informal soft ball league. The games were usually played a week after Captain's Inspection. Somebody was keeping a tally of who beat whom and at the end of the season there was usually a barbeque which occasionally turned into a Luau including young ladies dancing a hula. It was pleasant and took our minds off of some of our daily problems. Liberty was allowed from Saturday noon to Sunday at midnight for those who were not in the duty section.

A little ticked off at our suddenly curtailed liberty, Clyde, Sully, and I headed back to the Y and changed into our whites. Sully had grabbed a hamburger at the Black Cat Café and the aroma from it as he was eating made every body waiting for the bus or taxi a little hungry. A taxi pulled in, five of us piled in, and we headed back to Pearl. When we got to the base we went straight to the barracks and changed into our dungarees.

We had our bunks and lockers on the west wing of the top floor. The only time we slept on the boat was when we had the duty aboard or when we were out at sea. I remember we had a console model radio in our wing the movie people had donated to the crew for their cooperation during the filming of the movie *Submarine D-1* in San Diego. The radio was called a super-heterodyne receiver. It had one of those fancy tuning eyes enabling you to see how close you were to being correctly tuned in to a radio station.

After changing we headed down to the pier where the *Dolphin* was lying port side-to Sail Two, one of the five finger piers at the base. The *Narwhal* was tied up on the opposite side of the pier.

Chapter III: Whom Shall We Send

When Clyde, Sully, and I got down to the pier it looked like the *Dolphin* had come alive. Yard workers were swarming all over the ship. They looked much like ants in an ant farm. Welders were tacking something onto the conning tower, and electronic experts, (we called them Radar Technicians then) were installing some sort of antenna on top of the periscope shears. It turned out later to be the SD (Sugar Dog) radar. I had heard that they had installed an experimental set on the *USS Gar* a few months earlier back at Portsmouth Naval Shipyard in New Hampshire. The *Gar* was one of our newest boats. One of the men who reported aboard a few months earlier said that he had been aboard the *Gar* and by comparison to the *Dolphin*, he said it was luxurious. He said they had air conditioning built right in as a complete system whereas ours was a tacked on job that was so bad it only cooled the wardroom and part of the forward battery. When ever I had to go forward and pass through the forward battery I felt like I needed a jacket. The chiefs may have benefitted a little since their quarters were in the aft end of that compartment. But it was better than nothing. A side benefit was fewer electrical grounds in the forward battery well than in the after battery well. The constant dripping of the condensate from the air conditioning unit made the passageway slippery. The stewards mates had to keep swabbing the linoleum deck constantly to keep people from slipping.

We were being topped off with fuel from the barge alongside, and taking on fresh water from the lines on the pier. The water we received from Pearl was fine and sweet. The electricians were busy disconnecting the shore power lines. This alone proved to me that something very unusual was up, and the scuttlebutt that we would be in port for at least three weeks or more was not true. Something changed all that. Normally we would only connect to shore power if we were going to be tied up along side the pier for two weeks or more. It gave the Motor Machinists a break so they could work on the engines without the engine room getting so hot. Those engines always seemed to be needing work. If we didn't have shore power we would have had to use the engines to keep the batteries charged every fourth or fifth day or so depending on what kind of load we put on the battery.

I noticed that the hydraulic signal mast had been lowered and the attached halyards had been taken below and were stowed some where. I believe the mast was installed in the tube that would have contained a periscope issuing from the control room. We always had the mast up while in port to fly certain pennants such as Senior Officer Present Afloat, Broad and Burgee pennants plus first and second repeaters. We had to have an abundance of flags for almost every occasion. We flew one pennant that told everybody that the Captain was not aboard but would be back within 72 hours. The battleship admirals wanted submarines to have that ability to signal message receipts as all surface ships could.

Thank God that we didn't have to dismantle the awnings as we needed to in Panama. Those awnings were great for the top-side watch and for any of the crew either working or waiting for a liberty launch while it was raining. It rained frequently in the tropical atmosphere of the Panama Canal zone. This close to the equator the sun beat down on us severely and the awnings gave us show shadow effect but the heat still permeated the boat below decks. The awnings were a pain-in-the-ass to set up and take down. They consisted of pipe stanchions and braces with canvass stretched over them, providing shade from the hot tropical sun from over the four-inch deck gun, around the bridge, and aft over the topside torpedo storage and small boat locker. I think that was the main reason that we had a Boatswain's Mate as part of our crew; he had the skill to supervise this tedious work.

Dolphin in Panama Canal Zone

When I went below I inhaled the familiar and not totally unpleasant aroma of mineral spirits. The crew used rags containing spirits to wipe things down with rags. Things such as the brass and copper air, water and hydraulic lines had to be protected to try to slow down or control corrosion. I noted that most of our officers were in the Wardroom with papers spread out all over the table. The Yeoman was either typing something vigorously or running to and from our Division headquarters on the Tender, The *USS Pelias* (AS-13), with all kinds of papers and envelopes. He likely had various reports that were supposed to be sent off while we were going to be at sea, however long that was supposed to be. Every time he got back to the boat, it seemed that some officer would ask him to type up something else. He was one busy Yeoman. He was the *Dolphin's* secretary and typed all the ship's correspondence and reports. Yeomen were much maligned. Very few people would realize that many of them became first loaders on the four inch deck gun or part of the torpedo recovery team and that they had many other hazardous assignments during special evolutions. They didn't just type letters.

We were off-loading our exercise torpedoes and taking on war shot. That was unusual. We hardly ever carried fish with live warheads. Lately we had been carrying one war head in each torpedo room and not loaded in a tube. I guess that was to prevent an accidental firing at one of our targets. We had never carried a full load of torpedoes before and now we were fully loaded and none were "exercise fish". To me that was ominous especially since the war in Europe was in full swing. German U-Boats were raising havoc with the shipping in the Atlantic and it looked to me that our country might soon get involved. The United States had already taken 50 World War I four piper destroyers out of the mothball fleet in San Diego. After refurbishing they were loaned to Great Britain under the Lend Lease Act. The U.S. Navy's destroyer *Rubin James* had been torpedoed by a U-Boat and some so called neutral shipping had been sunk accidentally, so they said, by a U-Boat. The officers aboard were conspicuous in their silence. That added to the feeling we all had. Something very big was up for the *Dolphin* and her crew.

Clyde, Sully, and I joined the rest of the crew who were already hauling stores aboard from a couple of pick-up trucks and a large van-type truck that were parked on the pier. Loading stores is an all hands evolution. Every one, not on a major repair job or not on some errand that took them off the ship, was needed to bring the stuff aboard and stow it. Canned foods of all kinds; sugar, coffee and fruit juice, meat and vegetables. Loading stores is just plain boring and monotonous. Carrying all our provisions by hand across the narrow ribbed plank, called the brow, and down through the small hatches was exhausting. The brow stretched from the pier to our deck between the 4" deck gun and the forward radio mast stanchion. The cooks had the difficult job of telling everybody where and how to stow the food. How they managed to find time to cook a meal during loading is more than I could figure out.

There wasn't much in the way of frozen food in those days and what there was often had freezer burn. Even after cooking much of it was almost inedible. Of course we had our share of powdered milk and powdered eggs which most of us heartily disliked. Our food storage had a limited capacity and thus we had to stow the canned goods anywhere we could. Some of it right in the passage ways, and we had to walk on the boxes. I remember walking on cartons of canned peas, and some other cartons full of various canned foods for a couple of days until the cardboard started to come apart. By the third day we usually had consumed enough to get rid of the battered cartons and stow the rest out of the way in the store room.

The first two to three days at sea was hard on the mid-watch section, the crew that had the twelve to four watch. Each day the chief-of-the-boat, Chief Brown, would announce over the 1MC, "Up all bunks– All hands turn to on ship's work."

We would hold field day from 0800 till 1500 in the afternoon cleaning up the debris from all the stores we loaded which was mostly cardboard.. Every nook and cranny had to be swept clean. The guys that were on the mid-watch got little sleep.

We took a break before the evening meal and were standing around in the control room waiting for the second seating in crews mess, Sully asked me, "Hey Swede, how'd you like a drink of grapefruit juice?"

"Sounds good to me."

Sully handed me one of those large white navy mugs without handles. I savored the drink. I have always liked grapefruit juice. It felt good as it hit my stomach. Maybe that was the reason that I was never over-weight. I heard there was a grape fruit diet that was popular in the states. Without my asking, Sully gave me a refill right from the can. About half way through the second cup I started to feel dizzy. I started back to the head in the after battery. Somewhere en route I passed out. Half an hour later I woke up on my bunk. Some of my shipmates had laid me down in my bunk. I didn't drink at all in those days and I wasn't aware that Sully had spiked the drink with

"Gilley." Gilley was alcohol that was crudely distilled from the 200 percent torpedo alcohol and called "Pink Lady." The color denoted denatured alcohol and it was undrinkable. It would make you vomit. It was strong, about 200 proof and dangerous to your health. I heard that a couple of sailors lost their eyesight after drinking Gilley. Sully had poured most of the juice into another container, added a copious quantity of Gilley and filled up the can again with juice. To anyone looking, including me, he was just pouring juice out of the can. That's all any of the officers would ever see.

I took it easy after chow. Of course I had missed the meal. Later, when I felt I could navigate across the brow carrying some five-gallon cans of ground coffee aboard I continued to help loading the stores. We stored the coffee outboard of the engines. The five-gallon cans of sugar were stored in the motor room spaces. We finished around midnight and those of us that didn't have the duty went back up to the barracks and languished in the showers until we started to shrivel up. We wouldn't enjoy that luxury at sea for a long time with our limited water supply. Our evaporators produced potable water by using the heat of the engines exhaust but they had a very low capacity. There was no such thing as a salt water shower unless you got caught by an un-expected leak

We all hoped that we'd have time to get to the Ships Service Store, on the bottom floor of the barracks, to stock up on little goodies like Babe Ruth, Snickers, and Oh Henry candy bars. Wrigley's Juicy Fruit and Black Jack gum were popular. Magazines like *Colliers*, *Life*, *Liberty*, and *True Detective* helped to make life at sea a little more tolerable. Some of the guys would buy three cartons of Sea Stores cigarettes, the maximum you could buy, and they were cheap in those days. Ten cents a pack. Sea Stores cigarettes were available only to the people who would be out to sea for long periods of time. Incidentally Lucky Strike cigarettes came in a green package with Lucky Strike printed in black on a red circle whereas Chesterfields and Camels were in white packages. Some time after World War II started, Lucky Strike announced that some sort of chemical that was used to produce the green color of the package was vital to the manufacture of some munitions and that they were no longer going to come in that color. The old slogan, "It's Toasted", was replaced by "Lucky Strike green has gone to war" and the package was now white.

Lucky Strike Green has gone to war

I am glad that I didn't smoke in those days. The generally foul atmosphere in the boat after a prolonged dive was bad enough without adding cigarette smoke.

Something different was happening. I could tell it wasn't going to be our usual routine of two or three weeks at sea. For some reason I was sure we weren't going off on a simulated war patrol off Midway or Wake as we'd been doing for the past several months. What with all that activity and loading of all those stores in addition to torpedoes with war heads, the ship herself seemed to be trying to tell us something, but of course she had no way to tell us anything.

At 0700 the next morning at Quarters for Muster and Inspection, Lieutenant Bass, our Executive Officer, announced, "We will be getting underway at 1600 today. You'd better get any letters into the mail and if you need anything on the base you have only this morning to get it and tie up loose ends. All hands must be back aboard by 1300 and all departments will be ready for sea by 1400."

"Where are we headed?" asked someone in the back rank.

"All that type of information will be promulgated to you sometime after we get underway. Dismissed."

I'll never forget that date: Saturday, October 4, 1941.

Lt. Bass was a short, stocky, square built officer, slightly balding with a ruddy complexion. Mr. Bass was a Naval Academy graduate, class of 1931. We heard that he played football at the Academy and achieved national status as an All American. His sense of timing in everything he did told us he must have been one hell of a good player. He had just returned to us from a three week course on the new Torpedo Data Computer at Mare Island. Every submarine in the submarine force, including us, was supposedly going to get this new fire control device in the near future.

The Exec offered no word about where we were going or why the secrecy. The crew had great respect for Mr. Bass and trusted him totally. Even so, the anxiety of the crew was such that you could almost see the tension that was sparking among the men. Every body aboard relied on scuttlebutt to keep informed. I don't believe the Navy would be able to operate without scuttlebutt. If you're a fan of *MASH*, the sit-com on television, you know that Radar O'Reilly operated on the principle of scuttlebutt.

When the crew broke up after quarters they gathered in small groups all over the deck topside. I noticed Sully, Clyde, and a Fireman named Porky standing by the hatch leading down into the engine room. I headed over toward them.

As I got near Sully asked, "Hey, Swede. Have you heard anything at all?"

"Not a thing. How's about you guys?"

"That's what we're talking about. There's not even any scuttlebutt going around. We even quizzed the yeoman pretty hard. He said that he had no dope at all and I believe him."

Clyde spoke up. "Chief Brown has a friend over at the torpedo shop on the base, and he thought he would get a clue there but no dice."

"What the hell is going on, Swede?"

"I haven't a clue. We just have to wait it out and trust the skipper to let us in on whatever he can when he can."

"I ain't never bin in no place where there's bin no scuttlebutt afore. Makes me nervous," said Clyde.

"I think we ought to call the *Dolphin* 'USS Get Underway on Sunday.'"

"Why do you say that, Sully?"

"Because the last two times I was in the liberty section on a Sunday we had to get underway and I didn't get any time on the beach."

Porky added nothing. He just wagged his head, grunted and continued to gorge himself on a fat BLT sandwich he had just made in the galley despite the fact that it was only an hour or so after breakfast. It was obvious that all the other groups lingering about topside were engaged in the same type of conversation. We were all looking for some clue that we could hang our thoughts on. I was tense. I felt as if there were an electric charge traveling through the boat and that if I touched something or someone I'd get a shock.

Mr. Bass caught my eye and beckoned me over.

"Swenson, there's a package of charts ready to be picked up at the Division office. I'd like you get them for me."

"Aye, Aye, sir! I have the conning tower all squared away. I'll take care of that right away."

When I picked up the charts I asked the division Yeoman if he knew what was up and he said he had no idea what the plans were. Maybe he did and maybe he didn't so I headed back to the *Dolphin* with the charts tucked under my arm. They were rolled up tightly and held together with drafting tape so I couldn't even peek. That puzzled me even more. I usually had free access to all charts being as I normally had to stow them in the chart locker in the conning tower. My fingers were itching to peel back the tape to see what the charts covered, but I didn't dare with all the tension that was going around. I started to wonder if we were heading to a "Mysterious Island" or some other exotic place. I easily guessed that that would not be the case what with the loading of all those warheads. All twenty one of them including the three in the deck locker topside. Somebody wanted the *Dolphin* to be ready for *war*.

As I returned to her I stopped for a moment and gazed at the boat. She had the same general configuration as the newer boats. She had the same dull black paint all our submarines had. The color didn't show the grime as much as the light or battleship grey we had when we were in Panama and San Diego. We now sported the number 169 on the conning tower instead of the large black square with D-1 in white lettering on it. I noted that the number and the ship's name were being painted over. It seemed to me that someone didn't want the *Dolphin* to be easily identified. Why? Was it part of the realistic War Patrols around Midway Island again?

At 1600 the maneuvering watch was stationed and we were all set and ready to get underway. We had to wait for the Captain who, according to the Yeoman, was in conference with Commander Submarine Scouting Force Pacific, an Admiral, (After Pearl Harbor, that title changed to Commander Submarines Pacific). A meeting with the Division Commander was one thing but when you threw in the Squadron Commander and the Admiral in the same meeting, you knew that something extremely big was up. I wondered at the time if the Commander of the Pacific Fleet, Admiral Husband Kimmel, was also at that meeting

I remember thinking that it seemed peculiar to me that if this venture was so all fired, important why did they want us? The *Dolphin* was old and badly in need of an extensive overhaul. She was the third oldest of the twenty-two fleet type submarines assigned to Pearl Harbor. Only *Nautilus* and *Narwhal* were older but *Dolphin* was in far worse shape. *Nautilus* had departed from Pearl for Mare Island in California a few weeks earlier. She was getting a major overhaul along with three other of Pearl's fleet type boats. All of the six "S" class boats which were much older and smaller than *Dolphin* were in the San Diego; some in overhaul and some providing services to Anti-Submarine forces. The "S" boats had a much shorter range than the newer fleet boats.

The "Shark and Perch" classes plus the "Salmon, and Sargo" classes were shuffling through Pearl regularly. After a three week long war alert in late 1940 all of the Salmon class were sent to the Asiatic Fleet in Manila in the Philippine Islands. A lot of friends I had made were gone with them. The more modern boats didn't seem to stay at Pearl very long. The current thinking was that the Asiatic Fleet needed to be beefed up. If war was to start everybody seemed to think that is was going to start in Southeast Asia. We anticipated that the Pearl Harbor submarines would be increased in the near future. The submarine base seemed empty. Why send the old *Dolphin* out on a special mission? It looked to me that the *Dolphin* was the only one available. Perhaps the real reason the *Dolphin* was chosen was that it was expendable. I wondered if the crew was also thought to be *expendable*. Of course we were.

The *Dolphin* had two large direct drive diesel engines and two smaller but still large diesel engines running electric generators. She was 319 feet long, in part to accommodate the four big engines. They were the old M.A.N. diesels made under licence from the Germans. There were flaws in the design or else the blue prints the Germans provided our government had intentional mistakes in them. Perhaps they didn't want our engines to run as well as theirs. The engines never produced their rated horsepower and frequently broke down. It seemed that they couldn't take sustained use at high speeds.

The engines were idling. The maneuvering watch was stationed and standing at ease. The Captain, in uniform, and wearing a long sleeved khaki shirt and his customary black necktie, came striding down the pier and crossed over the brow saluting the colors and the deck watch. The deck watch was the equivalent of the Officer-of-the Deck on larger ships. The deck watch was supposed to be considered an officer, but he rarely was.

The Captain was carrying a large manilla envelope. As soon as he stepped aboard, the Yeoman handed our up-to-the-minute sailing list to the division Yeoman who was standing on the pier. The Navy had learned the hard way in the past that a last minute list of all people aboard was a very important detail in the event that some tragic accident or event occurred and the next of kin needed to be notified. That thought gave me the same feeling as the cloud shadow I felt on the beach the day before.

The Captain came up to the bridge and at the same time some sailors on the pier took the brow onto the pier. Normally we took in the brow and stowed it topside below the decking. That indicated to me that we were not going to tie up at another port for some time. That was hard for me to believe. The Captain gave the order to get underway. The Officer of the deck, Ltjg Holman ordered the deck gang to single up all lines. Then he had them take in the spring lines, numbers two and three lines, and then number four line aft.

He ordered, "All back one third," and sounded one long blast on the ship's whistle followed by three short blasts as we backed away from the finger pier out into the harbor taking in number one, the bow line, at the same time and ordering, "Secure topside for sea." We were underway with Mr. Holman at the conn.

The skipper, LCDR Rodney Malvern; Naval Academy class of 1925, wasn't tall. He was slim with a military posture. His eyes were blue and piercing and coupled with his black hair combed straight back, with no hint of a part, gave him a stern look. He always wore a necktie even while at sea. His thin face made him look austere. From his build I assumed that he was more of the academic type and made the assumption that he didn't participate in any athletics at the trade school as did our Executive officer. Like most of the Academy officers he probably concentrated on steam engineering and maintaining a high standing in his class.

The rest of our officers wore short sleeved khaki shirts without a tie while on the base or aboard ship. I am sure that the junior officers were happy that Captain Malvern did not impose his personal dress code on them. The only time that I remember the Captain saying anything about the officers' uniforms was when Mr. Holman got chewed out for cutting off the long sleeves of one of his khaki shirts. The Captain didn't mind the cutting, but insisted the sleeves be hemmed and not left ragged. We enlisted men wore white uniforms when we went on liberty in Hawaii and dungarees with white hats while aboard ship or on base.

A stickler for punctuality, the Captain seemed a trifle upset at getting under way at 1700, an hour later than planned. At "All ahead One third" we turned left past the Navy yard and headed out the channel. The *Dolphin* turned to port again at Hospital Point and with the main channel ahead we kicked our speed up to "All ahead Two thirds."

Topped off with fuel, food, water and with the trade winds kicking up a light froth on the sea, we headed out the channel. After passing 'Papa Hotel', an imaginary spot on the sea that marks the entrance to the Pearl Harbor channel, we increased our speed to, "All ahead Standard," and turned to 270 degrees true and headed west into a beautiful sunset.

As I watched the sun set I once again saw that brilliant, iridescent flash of blue-green light which occurs when the sun passes through the horizon in the tropics at sunset. Few people have seen it at all. I've seen it twice before. Each time I saw it, it seemed to me to have been an omen of good luck and I was its beneficiary. I had a stroke of good luck shortly after each sighting. I wondered what impact this flash of light would have on me this time considering the ominous preparations I witnessed prior to getting underway. I smugly assumed I would continue be the recipient of good luck again.

The vibrations from the throbbing engines were massaging my feet through the deck and the soles of my shoes. The gentle undulant swell of the ocean was soothing. I turned to check out the bridge. I noted that the signal light had been taken below and our running lights were all properly lit. The gyro compass repeater and the rudder angle indicator seemed to be working okay. Taking a deep breath of clear, sweet smelling salt air I went below.

The evening meal consisted of Salisbury Steak, smothered in onions with green beans and topped off with a slice of apple pie. I'd have liked a scoop of ice cream on top of the pie but the electricians had disconnected the ice cream machine. After super, I poured myself a cup of strong coffee properly enhanced with four heaping teaspoons of sugar and enough evaporated milk to make it look like light chocolate. It's hard to believe but our coffee urn had a twenty five gallon capacity and coffee was re-brewed four or five times every twenty four hours. After ensuring that my coffee was just right I went back up to the conning tower.

Checking the previous watches log, I noticed that Mr. Holman had written, "The *Dolphin* set sail at 1700 hours."

The phrases, "set sail" or "we sailed" always bugged me ever since I enlisted in the Navy. US Navy ships hadn't had sails for over thirty years except for the *Constitution* our oldest commissioned ship. Mr. Holman should have used the proper term "got underway." I put away the charts of Pearl Harbor which I assumed we wouldn't be using for some time. The conning tower needed some general straightening up. That done I went below and thought briefly about writing a letter to Meilin. But I hit the sack instead and promptly fell sound asleep.

Chapter IV: Underway

The first morning at sea there was an electrical short circuit in our interior communications motor generator system. It plunged the ship into total darkness below decks for about an hour. The electricians, working with the light from our emergency battle lanterns, got the problem solved. It was a simple electrical connection that had come apart and one wire had fallen across another. It was caused by a corroded joint. It seemed that almost all of our equipment, electrical or mechanical, had corroded to some extent.

I had the eight to twelve watch and spent most of it on the bridge. We made our first trim dive since we loaded all those stores and had the extra antennas installed. The dive was about as standard as you can get and Mr. Molloy obtained a satisfactory trim in less than an hour. Not bad for a first dive after taking on that additional weight of stores and torpedoes. He adjusted the variable trim tanks by pumping or flooding sea water in and out and fore and aft as well. We were close to neutral buoyancy plus or minus a few hundred pounds and had a good fore and aft balance. Captain Malvern ordered Mr. Molloy to make our depth 250 feet, our test depth. We did that the first time at sea after being in port to check for any major leaks. No problems of any kind developed. As usual, sonar made several sweeps around at 200 and 100 feet. Sonar reported no contacts. We returned to periscope depth and finding no ships near by, surfaced.. We settled down into our underway routine.

The following morning I once again had the watch when we made our daily trim dive. As usual, I was the first man on the bridge when we surfaced, followed quickly by the Captain and two lookouts. My job was to take a quick look around and report if it was all clear close aboard when the Captain reached the bridge. My binoculars had fogged up and I headed back down to the conning tower to get another pair. I felt the *Dolphin* start to take on a down angle. Suddenly the Captain and lookouts came scrambling down off the bridge right. They were followed by green water pouring through the hatch.

"Dog the hatch!" shouted the Captain.

I didn't need to be ordered to do that. I had the hatch dogged securely before the Captain finished his order. The four of us were drenched. The boat leveled out and no longer appeared to be sinking. It began to rise as we heard the noise of the high pressure air once again blowing into the ballast tanks. Mr. Holman poked his head up into the conning tower and sheepishly told us that they hadn't shut the vent valves when we surfaced. Our Kingston valves were locked open when we rigged for dive. All that kept us afloat on the surface was the air in the ballast tanks held in there by the vent valves. Open the vent valves and the submarine sinks. Blowing the tanks would cause us to surface but with the vents still open the air quickly escaped. Now, back on the bridge we could hear the low pressure blowers screaming air into the ballast tanks.

Once again on the surface we discovered, much to Captain Malvern's disgust, that we had left a third lookout up on the bridge when we began to submerge. I didn't have time to count the men as they came below. It was an Electrician's mate by the name of Johnson. He managed to hang on to the periscope at the top of the shears. Sopping wet, looking pale and obviously scared to death, we sent him below. If we had continued to submerge we might not have found him and he might not have survived for very long. The Captain was furious. I didn't want to be in Mr. Holman's shoes that afternoon. I'm sure that he got a real chewing out. I lucked out on that one because my job was to count the men coming down. I didn't do that this time. Why? Was it too fast? I don't make mistakes like that. I wondered if this was a hint of what we had to look forward to on this patrol. What about my good luck omen? The flash of blue-green light.

Subsequently, we made a few more dives to ensure that that mistake was never repeated. We learned that lesson the hard way and it was imbedded in our brains from then on. To me the incident didn't bode well since at least ninety percent of the officers and crew were seasoned, qualified men. A mistake like that should never have happened in the first place. We had made hundreds of dives and that had not ever happened before. The thought occurred to me that the Christmas tree may have indicated the vents were shut when they really weren't. I became suspicious of the Christmas tree lighting circuitry. Had it gone bad because of corrosion or something?

The next few days were uneventful with most of it spent speculating on where we were heading and why. Aside from our daily trim dive the trip, so far, was boring. The lookouts and OOD scanned the horizon with their binoculars from the bridge. There were no contacts to report. At the end of watch, Ding-Dong came up and relieved me as Quartermaster-of- the-watch. I took a long look at the sun hanging low in the sky surrounded by heavy looking clouds and went below to partake of one of Belly Robber Rick's better meals; Chicken Fried steak. He did a nice job adding a good gravy with peas and carrots on the side. It was tasty and filling. The sailors aboard *Dolphin* had a saying that caught on with other submarines in Pearl Harbor:

"She's not much on liberty but she sure is a good feeder."

Our cooks were damn good.

After the evening meal I headed back up to the conning tower and did a little clean up. After putting stuff back where it belonged, I stepped over and looked up the hatch.

I asked, "Permission to come to the bridge, sir?"

"Permission granted."

On the bridge, I took a few deep breaths of fresh air. A crescent moon barely lit the darkening, oily looking sea.. The ocean had picked up considerably since my last watch and the swell had become more pronounced. The sky was thick with large, dark clouds and it looked as if the weather was going to get worse. I didn't look forward to going on watch that night;.I knew it was going to be a rough one.

After a few brief words with the Officer of the Deck, I took a quick look around the bridge and then, with permission, I dropped down below into the conning tower to chat with 'Ding-Dong' a little bit about surfing. 'Ding-Dong' was the ships resident surfing champion. He spent all of his time ashore surfing somewhere off Oahu.

"Ding-Dong, have you ever seen any sharks while you were surfing?"

"No. I never have and I don't expect to. You're going too fast and they got better things to eat than skinny guys like me."

The Officer-of-the Deck called down for Ding-Dong to come to the bridge. That terminated our conversation. I had a fascination with the elasmobranch fishes (sharks) and later did some extensive research on them. I checked the Captain's Night Order book for anything that I might need to know for my next watch and then went below. It was a habit I developed that helped me greatly later on when I was commissioned and stood watches as officer of the deck. I always knew what the Captain's intentions were and was prepared to deal with them. That habit helped me sleep rather comfortably at night. I always knew when we were planning to dive or start a battery charge and the sound of an engine starting up was merely a reminder that things were normal. I would turn over and go back to sleep.

Sully, who was finishing his dinner with a large brownie and a cup of coffee, looked up as I passed through the crew's mess:

"Any word yet on where we're heading, Swede?"

"Not a word, Sully. No one's talking. I might get a clue later when I go back up to the wardroom to wind the chronometers."

The ship's master chronometers had to be wound daily and had to be compared to Greenwich Mean Time by means of a time-tic which our radio shack got by radio from the Naval Observatory. The chronometers were in a cabinet in the after end of the ward room. A report was made to the commanding officer, daily at 1600. "All chronometers have been wound and compared." It was also included in the 1200 report to the Captain.

"You Quartermasters always get the poop before us peons do, so keep us informed. OK?"

"I always do, Sully."

Three officers were sitting at the wardroom table, talking over coffee. I knocked on the bulkhead and asked for permission to wind the chronometers. They stopped talking and nodded an OK. They resumed talking when I finished but I couldn't hang around to listen to what they were saying without being conspicuous. Sully was gone when I got back to the after battery but I had no news for him any way. I got my writing gear out from under my mattress and headed back to crew's mess. It had been cleaned up by the mess cooks by then so I could use the mess tables to write to Meilin. I felt sure I would be able to mail the letter when we got to Midway.

Dear Meilin, my little Eskimo

I'm so very sorry that I wasn't able to call you but we had to get out to sea right away and we don't know why. It must be some special exercise. I'll mail this to you when we get to where ever they send us if we don't come back to Pearl. I would tell you where we are going if I knew but I don't. I promised to take you out to dinner Saturday night but I will have to do that when I get back. I'll make it up to you some time, some how. You never know where or why the Navy sends you or how long we will be gone.

    Ho. Ts'oi kin
    Your special friend,
    Eric

At Quarters the other morning I had heard the Exec say that we should get any letters into the mail but I stubbornly refused to believe we really wouldn't be able to mail a letter. Surely we would be putting into Midway or Wake or possibly Guam in a week or so. Stuffing the letter in my folder and replacing it under my mattress in the after battery, I hit the sack.

The next morning with breakfast finished, I went up into the conning tower and checked the Dead-Reckoning Tracer. The track showed that we were not heading for Midway as I had assumed. Why? Something peculiar was going on. We could have been headed to Panama or Alaska for all I knew, except the compass indicated that we were heading west and Panama was southeast and Alaska was north. I guess I had subconsciously assumed that we were going to be on another simulated patrol off Midway. Maybe the war in Europe had taken a bad turn. The rolling of the ship told me that the weather had livened up. It had become rough. I put on my foul weather jacket and climbed onto the bridge.

The weather had indeed gotten worse. The waves were topped with fringes of white foam and the wind was about 20 knots. While taking it all in, I struck up a conversation with Ltjg Holman, the OOD.

"Aren't we going to put in to Midway, Mr. Holman?"

"No', we're heading for Wake." he said adding, "The *Dolphin* likes to be different."

"How come?"

"I don't know. Besides, the Captain hasn't tucked us in on our orders yet. Don't start spreading any scuttlebutt around on that. You'd get me in trouble with the Captain if you did."

"The crew is sure anxious to get some info."

"All I can say is Captain Malvern told us that we were heading for Wake. We'll all get the scoop when the Captain's ready."

"I won't say anything, sir."

"Thank you."

The rest of the watch proved uneventful.

The next morning we made our usual trim dive. On surfacing in the trough of a heavy swell one of the racks, holding a torpedo in the forward room, came loose. The roll caused the rack to shift and it might have crushed anyone in its way as it slid across the room. We weren't worried about a possible detonation of the torpedo because they were very safe to handle unless they were armed. The dogs that held the rack in place were quite well worn and had slipped out of their grooves. The Torpedo men ended up lashing all racks tightly. At the time I asked myself, If we were at war and had to reload a torpedo now, how much longer would it take to unlash the racks in order to line them up for a reload? I'll bet it would use up a lot of valuable time. Those worn dogs had been high on our list of recommended repairs.

When I got off watch I dropped down into the conning tower and cleaned my binoculars. I took very good care of them. Stashing them in a small locker I had made by the shipyard the last time we were in overhaul, I dropped down into the control room and headed aft to the galley. I drew a cup of coffee and sat down to relax. Some of the torpedo men were there trying to get the flush of adrenalin to subside. They were keyed up and all talking at once. At times their job could be exciting as well as dangerous.

During the next several days we experienced a sharp drop in our fresh water supply since leaving Pearl. The potable water capacity is monitored on a daily basis by the Auxilliaryman of the watch. After having the Machinists's Mates check the fresh water system for leaks the Chief-of-the Boat, Brown, ordered a couple of the mess cooks monitor our two showers twenty four hours a day. Adrian Stark, a rosy cheeked, fattish, tender young Yeoman striker who had reported aboard just out of submarine school at New London, was found to be enjoying long showers late at night. Chief Brown, a powerfully built, muscular man of 28 years who looked like he could carry a twenty one foot long torpedo under each arm with ease, ordered the culprit brought to the chief's quarters. The chief scowled at him fiercely:

"Stark! What do you mean by taking long showers every night? Don't you know our water supply is limited?"

Visibly nervous and shaking, Stark stammered:

"Yes sir."

"Don't sir me, Stark. I ain't no officer. What's your excuse for wasting water?" he growled.

"I...I...forgot my Mum."

"Mum? What the hell is Mum?"

"My ah...my underarm deodorant," Stark rapidly spit out.

"You forgot to bring along underarm deodorant? What the hell do you think you're on, a cruise liner or sumpin?"

"No."

"No, what?"

"Ah,...er no, chief"

"Don't let me catch you wasting water again. Is that clear?"

"Yes, sir, Chief."

"Dam it! I said Don't 'sir' me. Don't you ever listen? You're dismissed."

Stark, appropriately chastised, left the chief's quarters with his tail between his legs.

Our weekly showers consisted of turning on the shower, getting wet, shutting off the water, soaping down and then rinsing off. A minimal use of water. Many of the crew grew beards and gave as the excuse that they were conserving water. Captain Malvern frowned on beards and soon forbade them. He said this was the modern navy not the nineteenth century. He added that we weren't pirates either. The beards were soon gone.

We continued to plough through the Pacific at about 12 knots; our most economical speed on the surface. Other than routine trim dives that occurred every other day nothing broke the monotony except when the Pharmacists Mate reported that Peters, our 2nd class Gunners Mate, had a very severe pain in his abdomen that might be appendicitis. There was no way we could handle that kind of problem aboard the *Dolphin*. Scuttlebutt now reared its ugly head. It said that we would return to Pearl Harbor. We didn't turn back. I wondered why? Were we on a specific time table? What was so urgent?

About this point in time we would normally have been putting into Midway, we crossed the international date line. In addition to changing our clocks to coincide with local time zones, we now gained a day. It created griping amongst the crew, especially among the Motor Machinists in the engine rooms. There are three time zone changes between Pearl Harbor and Wake Island and each zone added an hour to each of the daily watches. The guys complained when I set the clocks ahead each time. I told them they'd lose an hour on the way back but that didn't seem to stop the complaining. I took a lot of flak over that. One of the Motor Machinist Mates asked:

"What if we don't go back? We could be heading around the world."

I couldn't answer him. Maybe he had a point.

Silence prevailed for the rest of the week. No word over the 1-MC, no notice posted, no scuttlebutt; and that was unusual. Scuttlebutt was usually dependable and prevalent most of the time, but there was absolutely none so far on this trip. We didn't know why. That bothered all of us. What were they hiding? Was it something we should know or would just like to know? There was a tangible uneasiness in the crew. You couldn't define it but it was there.

A normal report would be given in a terse, clipped voice and the recipient would say something like, "Who do you think you are, a chief?"

Reactions weren't the same. It was not normal and I based it on all the secrecy that surrounded us. The lack of scuttlebutt.

On the morning of the sixth day at sea, a lookout spotted a navy flying boat on the horizon. I think he said it was a Catalina. A PBY. We knew we were getting close to Wake Island and finally it appeared on the horizon, highlighted by a few cumulus clouds. A slight error in navigation and we would have missed it. We anchored on the Southwest side of Wilkes Island and then waited for the Port Captain to show up.

While we were waiting I raised the periscope and took a look at this atoll. At high tide you could see almost the entire island from *Dolphin's* bridge. That is, all three islands that make up Wake. Peale, Wilkes, and Wake. I have never seen a more desolate place than Wake. Wake had nothing but some kind of low scrub trees and some scraggly shrubs. It was in no way one of those palm covered islands you saw in the Dorothy Lamour–Bob Hope movies. It made me more claustrophobic than a submarine ever did. It's a tad better than Midway, though. Midway had fewer trees and seemed to be largely sand. It also had a large colony of Gooney Birds which were quite amusing in their clumsy antics on the land compared to their beautiful soaring in the air. Watching them trying to take off from the beach was really funny. Midway was good for swimming in the lagoon. The water looked tempting here at Wake. It was conducive for swimming but we were told we couldn't. Most likely because we weren't going to be there long enough. Later I understood that side of the island wasn't good for swimming anyway. Too many sharks they said.

A small harbor craft came along side and the port captain, a civilian, came aboard. He told us that they were prepared to fuel us but that we would have to wait until their utility boat could get through the small dredged channel. The utility boat would tow the floating diesel line out to *Dolphin* and the civilian craft would then be used to keep us from swaying excessively in the swells while we were taking on the diesel oil. It didn't take long before we started topping off with diesel fuel. I gathered from Sully the reason we stopped for fuel was they were not sure of the consumption rate of our diesels. It turned out to be fine but later we were to thank God that we had topped off. I didn't think, however, we had used very much fuel from Pearl Harbor to Wake.

The port captain told us that we couldn't take on any fresh water because Wake's supply was reserved for the use of Pan American Clipper passengers during their stop over en-route to Guam, the Philippines, and Singapore. What a lousy break for us. That Yeoman striker, Stark, caused all of us to lose some shower time.

The Captain came up to the bridge and told us that the Pharmacist's Mate needed to send our Gunner's Mate, Gil Peters, ashore for transfer back to Pearl harbor. It seems that Peters was running a high fever and was diagnosed as having acute appendicitis. The control room called up for permission to open the after battery hatch so they could get him out easily. Permission was quickly granted.

A flurry of activity took place with the Boatswain's Mate and a couple of guys rigging the twenty two foot long boom; the same boom and jib we used for loading our torpedoes. Then un-sealing the locker that contained our small, outboard powered, boat. The steel container was mounted directly aft of the conning tower and just above the topside spare torpedo storage. We could carry three extra torpedoes intended to supplement the after tubes since they only had two tubes aft. They were a bitch to maneuver to the after torpedo room loading hatch in anything but the calmest of weather. We did that only once off San Diego and it didn't go very well. We almost lost a torpedo. Wrenches were needed to unbolt the lid. It took about twenty minutes to get the boat out of the container and into the water. Another five minutes were needed to mount and start the outboard motor. Everyone was surprised when it started right up. It usually required about ten minutes of trying before it fired off.

By then the Pharmacist's Mate had Peters out on deck. Peters, doubled over in pain, was patiently waiting for the ladder to be rigged out. We had a ladder built into the deck superstructure that folded outboard. It helped people getting on or off the ship. "Doc" helped Peters into the boat and stayed with him on the trip over to the base. Our Boatswain's mate was handling the craft and headed it through the small channel and over to the China Clipper base inside the lagoon. About a twenty minute trip one way. During World War II there were at least three cases of appendicitis, maybe more, and one that I know about was a man who was operated on during a war patrol. The operation was successful but ComSubPac frowned on that practice and forbid the boats from doing it. Pharmacists were instructed to use medication and the commanding officer was required to transfer the patient to another ship or a base at the earliest possible time.

Our small boat got back shortly before we completed topping off with fuel. "Doc" told us that Peters would probably be getting a ride on a Clipper back to Pearl Harbor. "Lucky" Peters. That's a laugh. None of us would have enjoyed having our appendix removed just to get a free flight on a China Clipper. It probably cost the Government a bundle of money but to Peters it was free. The Boatswain and a couple of the men stowed the small boat again and tightly bolted the small boat container. They stored the davit and gear in the topside lockers. The after battery hatch was shut. Topside was secured for sea and the men went below. With Peters gone and our refueling completed, we became aware of the heat and humidity. The *Dolphin's* small air conditioning unit didn't do us much good. Stationing the Maneuvering watch once again, we cast off the civilian small craft's lines and weighed anchor. Backing out into deeper water we were underway again minus one sailor. I was sure glad to get away from Wake Island. We droned along to our unknown destination, diving once a day to maintain our trim. All we knew was that we were heading west; China or possibly Japan. Maybe even Guam. It was rather pleasant at sea as the Pacific Ocean lived up to its name - peaceful. The swell and the wind had subsided. Drills were sporadic.

Two days out of Wake we had a scare. We were making our usual morning trim dive and shortly after starting to submerge, the klaxon sounded three blasts; the signal to surface. That was unusual. I heard the high pressure air blowing into the ballast tanks. Roused from my sleep at an unusual occurrence, I raced forward from my bunk to the control room. I heard shouting about flooding. I damn near panicked. The high induction (later called the main induction) had failed to shut. That meant "emergency surface." The Christmas tree indicated that the valve was shut. The Christmas tree is a panel mounted above and in back of the hydraulic manifold. It shows a green light for every hull opening that is shut and a red light for every one remaining open. Any red light on the board indicates an opening that, if left open, could flood and sink us. We had to have a "Green board" before diving.

The diving officer, Mr. Ward, had been alert and had caught the problem quickly enough to correct it. We recycled the main induction valve several times to insure it was working again. Then we had the job of pumping out the water that had flooded into the engine rooms. A branch of the induction piping, called the low induction, had an outlet into the radio trunk which also flooded and grounded out almost every circuit connected with our communications equipment . That kind of excitement I could do without. The radiomen had a long, tough time getting the radio circuits dried out and partially working again. They never were able to totally correct all the grounds.

Standard procedure upon hearing the diving klaxon was for the chief-of-the-watch to observe the Christmas tree and when he sees nothing but green lights on it immediately opens all main ballast tank vent valves. He then opens an air valve and bleeds air into the boat. He watches the manometer and if it remains steady he calls out "Green board - pressure in the boat", and the dive continues. If the manometer reading falls it indicates that a major hull opening is flooding the boat and the dive is stopped. The chief makes sure that the vent valves are shut. The diving officer orders all ballast tanks blown plus negative tank which provides negative buoyancy upon diving. In this case Mr. Ward and Chief Walton who was chief-of-the-watch saw the main induction light turn green but the air pressure didn't remain steady so they blew the tanks immediately. Something had to be wrong with Christmas tree circuits in my opinion.

All of us, from the Captain on down, were reminded of the *Squalus* disaster in 1939. The *Squalus* also had a main induction failure while making a dive while on builders trials. They had made several successful dives previously. For some reason they didn't or couldn't blow ballast tanks and the boat plunged to the bottom. Thirty three men were saved but twenty six were lost. They sank in 220 feet of water. The water where we were was over 3000 feet deep. The *Squalus* had rescue vessels within 100 miles while we were about 1600 miles from any help. We couldn't possibly have been saved. It took three days to save the men aboard *Squalus* and some of those rescued had spent as long as forty hours on the bottom. As I recall it was also the first use of the new McCann Rescue Chamber.

The hull of *Dolphin* would have been crushed between 400 and 500 feet. My stomach was tied up in knots and I broke out into a cold sweat. The Squalus disaster occurred shortly after I had enlisted in the Navy but that didn't deter me from getting into submarines. I later found out the *U.S.S. Snapper (SS-185)* had the same problem and survived.. I also heard the *U.S.S. Sturgeon (SS-187)*, another submarine of the same class, had a similar experience in about the same time frame.

TOP SECRET

Our usual routine would be broken once in a while when a lookout would shout, *"Plane!"* and we would make a quick dive. We headed deep to 100 feet. Captain Malvern came into the control room when he heard the diving alarm. He ordered periscope depth and took a look around. Seeing nothing he surfaced the boat. Once on the surface, an event such as this, usually revealed the "plane" was an Albatross or some other sea bird. We submerged because the one thing that did come out about our orders was we had been told to remain undetected by any air or surface craft including our own. Another event that would break the monotony would be when a lookout's call would be *"Periscope"* and we'd dive. Most likely the lookout had seen a glint of light from the sun on the water or perhaps off of a glass bottle floating in the water. When we were on the surface at night our running lights were extinguished and the fuses pulled . That one little fact was the only hint we had as to what our mission might be. That surely meant, to me, that our operation had to be "Top Secret".

One morning, on the eight to twelve watch, the skipper finally let the cat out of the bag. He used the 1 MC to announce to the crew what our mission was.

"This is the Captain speaking. I know all hands have been wondering about our mission. I can now tell you that we have been assigned the task of monitoring Japanese Naval operations on the south east coast of the Japanese Island of Kyushu. We are to observe all naval activities including, in particular, any large amphibious operations. We are to remain undetected at all times. I don't expect us to remain on station for more than fifteen days. Your worry over the lack of scuttlebutt should now be put to rest. That is all."

Now I knew why the Captain didn't tell us sooner. He didn't want to take the chance someone might leak information about our mission while we were at Wake. It pleased me to know that Captain Malvern was aware that we were all concerned about the lack of scuttlebutt. We knew that the Japanese were on the offensive in Manchuria and Japanese aircraft had sunk the river gunboat *U.S.S. Panay (PR-5)* in 1937 more than five years after the *Dolphin* was commissioned. I guess our spies had picked up some information that needed to be verified and we had to check it out. We were to become spies ourselves.

I wondered then, why we hadn't stopped at Midway. On a great circle route a stop at Midway would have been shorter. So why stop at Wake? Why didn't we stop at Midway? The amount of diesel oil we took aboard was relatively small. That fact deepened the mystery of our mission to me. The only men, not even the Captain, who got off the boat at Wake were the Doc with Peters and the Boatswains mate. None of them knew what our orders were. Maybe that was the real reason why we weren't allowed to go swimming while we were anchored there.

Three days out of Wake we passed about seventy five nautical miles south of Marcus Island, a Japanese Mandated island. We had to be very careful during this transit because we didn't know whether they had any aircraft or warships operating out of there. Three or four days later we passed through the widest gap in the Bonin Island chain, and incidentally we were within 50 miles of what later became the site of a major World War II battle in the Pacific. *Iwo Jima*. I still have a copy of the note to the captain stating that Iwo Jima was forty six nautical miles directly south of us.

Mid-morning, about two days later, we made landfall on Tanega Shima, a small island due south of Kyushu; one of the main Japanese islands. We had to go around it to enter a strait called the strait of Van Diemen. Today that strait is called Osumi Kaikyo. We submerged because the Captain said we were so close to the heavily populated Japanese islands there was a good chance we could be detected by aircraft. Captain Malvern insisted that we go to 120 feet because of the likelihood of Japanese aircraft in the area. He said there was a high probability aircraft could see us or our shadow cast by our hull when the sun was at the right angle.

We surfaced after sunset and commenced recharging our batteries. It was raining heavily as we cruised south west through the straits. We barely made out the mast head and running lights of a large ship heading toward us and we made a quick dive. The term "crash dive" wasn't used until early 1942 and then mostly by the Hollywood film makers. The rain had made the bridge slippery. On every dive as quartermaster of the watch, I was supposed to be the first one down, count the crew as they came down off the bridge to make sure that we didn't leave anyone topside and stand by to dog the hatch as soon as the OOD slammed it shut. This time I leapt for the hatch, hit the ladder and half way down I slipped. Every one on the bridge, all four of them, the three lookouts and the OOD, landed on my legs as I lay sprawled on the deck at the foot of the ladder. I barely managed to get up on my feet to dog the hatch. There was no doubt in my mind that everyone on the bridge was down and accounted for. I had counted each one as they landed on me. My legs were terribly painful and bloody. It's a wonder I didn't have both my legs broken. I have scars on both legs to this very day from that crazy episode.

The lookouts proceeded to drop down into the control room to take their stations at the bow and stern plane controls and operate them. They had large thirty inch in diameter wheels with which they controlled the planes and large shallow water depth gauges to guide them. There was a built in level with a bubble in it to indicate the trim of the boat. The helmsman stayed at the wheel in the conning tower. We normally took about 60 seconds to dive and made it easily in that amount of time. We didn't have the margin of safety we would have liked to have had. The range to the oncoming ship was closing so rapidly that it was a close call. Diving time, for most boats, later during the war would approach thirty seconds to get under to periscope depth. I wondered at the time why we hadn't been using our SD radar.

We reached the ordered 120 foot depth and leveled off. We could clearly hear through the hull the loud, crunching, cement mixer noise of multiple propellers churning through the water. The noise grew louder and we went deeper to 200 feet. The sound quickly faded as the ship passed over. We stayed deep for about an hour. After we surfaced, I heard the Captain say it sounded to him like an aircraft carrier or a battleship but we couldn't confirm it because of the darkness and the rain, and because we were at or below 120 feet at the time. The Captain added that it couldn't possibly have been a merchant ship.

The job of shutting and dogging the hatch was extremely important. The Quartermaster of the watch had to be alert to see that the hatch was indeed seated and hadn't bounced up a half inch or two because if the dogs were extended as you tried to close the hatch and even sea pressure would not seal the gap no matter how hard you tried or how deep you went. On the other hand you had to watch for sandals that had slipped off or keys that were dropped that could also keep the hatch from seating on its rim. Many conning towers have been at least partially flooded by events like that. Some of the men would cut off the heel straps of their sandals and occasionally they would fall off as they raced for the hatch. The next morning we arrived off our destination, Kagoshima Wan (Kagoshima Bay) on the southern tip of Kyushu. I believe the Japanese used a contraction for the name of this bay. The Japanese called it Kinkowan. This location is about a 100 miles, as the crow flies, from one of the two cities in Japan that became well known toward the end of the war. Hiroshima and Nagasaki. They were destroyed by the Atomic bomb that was dropped on them

Chapter V: On Station

Submerged at periscope depth in the straits outside of Kagoshima Wan, Captain Malvern was attempting to get the surroundings of the bay well in mind before trying to investigate the area. While we were making one of our periscope observations, the Sonar operator called up to the conning tower from his station in the forward torpedo room. He reported there were multiple high speed screws astern coming on rapidly. Sonar believed they were approaching from the east. From his vantage point, with the scope only a foot or so out of the water, Captain Malvern could not see any ships. We reversed course, went deep and headed farther into the straits to check out the source of the sound. Slowing down and coming back up to periscope depth the Captain took another look around. He stopped during his search, slapped up the handles of the scope and immediately ordered, "Down scope, make your depth 125 feet"

A few minutes later the Captain addressed the Executive officer. I was standing at the Captain's elbow:

"Lt. Bass, we have a large aircraft carrier out there and it's launching planes."

"Yes, sir."

"The carrier is accompanied by at least two destroyers and possibly a third acting as a plane recovery unit."

"Yes, sir."

"Even though the carrier is pulling out of sight, I want you to place a note in our standard operating procedures to the effect that while we are submerged in these waters we will stay at 125 feet except during periscope observations."

"Consider it done, sir."

He again expressed his concern that the aircraft in their landing pattern might detect us. He said that we would remain at 125 feet for awhile. I couldn't imagine any pilot trying to land on what must seem to be as large as a postage stamp in the middle of the ocean (an aircraft carrier) would have the time or the inclination to study the water below for any shadows that might disclose a lurking submarine, but then I was not the skipper. I noted the observation of the carrier in the log book. While writing these new orders in the log the idea started to sink into my brain that we must be on a very serious mission.

An hour after the propellor noises from the carrier faded out, the Captain ordered periscope depth. After taking a slow, careful look all around he dipped the scope, raised it once again and looked back toward our objective. He said it was difficult to tell it was a bay because its wide mouth extended about eight miles or more. On both sides of the bay there were tall peaks that looked like they could have been volcanoes at one time. The snow frosted mountains were covered with what seemed to be lush vegetation below the snow line. We headed into the bay. Our charts were old and poor. We weren't sure of the best way to enter the bay. Captain Malvern decided to try the southeastern side first.

During this approach we were plagued by a large number (the Captain used the word hundreds) of small fishing sampans. From the Captain's point of view it became very tedious trying to thread our way through the armada of small boats. A wind had come up and churned the water somewhat which helped hide our periscope when we looked around. The wind also blew away the cloud cover and the slight haze that had gathered. On one occasion Captain Malvern lingered at the scope for a full minute. (Periscope exposures of more than ten to fifteen seconds were frowned on by all squadron commanders in the submarine force.) He said that the mountains to the north west of us were like those on a picture post card for tourists. He told us it was beautiful. He finally ordered the scope lowered.

Dodging the sampans became a real chore. They seemed to have gathered in small fleets. One group had a bearing drift to the right and another seemed to have a bearing drift to the left. It took at least two observations on each group to determine their drift rate so we could figure out the best course to get past them. I wondered at the time that if the Captain was so worried about us or our shadow being seen by aircraft, wasn't there a possibility of the fishermen also seeing our shadow or even our hull since we were only fifty feet or so below them and in crystal clear water? Weren't they engaged in looking down into the water for fish?

The increasingly choppy seas made our periscope observations more difficult. We had to put more of the scope up than we would like to expose. Late in the afternoon, we headed back into the straits and again dropped down to 120 feet. After surfacing that night to charge batteries, dump trash and garbage, and blow sanitary tanks, we found fishing nets tangled all over the bridge, deck, radio masts, and the four inch deck gun. Lt. Molloy and a crew of his engineers, all wearing life jackets, went topside to evaluate the situation. They sent some of the men below to get axes and bolt cutters to cut them off. We sure were lucky they didn't get tangled up in our propellers. The nets were held up with hollow glass balls anywhere from three or four to twelve inches in diameter instead of the cork floats that American fishermen used. All of us, officers and men alike, collected the globes as souvenirs. While the topside crew were cleaning up the mess, we took several soundings to ensure we had sufficient water below us to dive safely if we had to.

The next morning we headed toward the center of the bay. To help pin-point our position we made several passes across the entrance for any indication of what might be the best course to enter the broad bay. With the absence of any military or other shipping the Captain ordered soundings and the fathometer was turned on as we proceeded to enter the bay again. Had we been at war, we probably would not have used the fathometer because it did make an audible noise. We were at 50 feet, our periscope depth, and the soundings came up into the conning tower every minute. As I recall they started out at about twenty fathoms, which meant that there was 120 feet of water under our keel. The soundings came rapidly.

"19 fathoms, 16 fathoms, 13 fathoms, 12 fathoms."

We were shoaling fast. Captain Malvern ordered right full rudder and reversed course. He always became very nervous when he couldn't get down to at least 120 feet and, in his words, "be safe from detection by aircraft."

In several days we made more attempts to enter the bay from various points and discovered that the bay had essentially two channels; one on the northwest side and one on the southeast. The center section was extremely shallow; characteristic of most river deltas. I was sure that this was the case. Farther up in the bay what looked like a small, apparently dormant, volcano seemed to be separating the two channels. We found out later that the southeastern channel didn't reach all the way into the bay. There was an isthmus stretching between the volcano and the main land on the east side.

After spending an entire day probing the entrance to the bay we headed back out to the straits. We came to periscope depth and looked around. The sun had set and a fog was starting to form. We surfaced and commenced performing our usual routine. Visibility had been reduced to about 1000 yards. We started a battery charge but deferred the dumping of trash and garbage. The Captain didn't want a lot of men on the bridge with the possibility of having to dive at any second. No star sights were possible but we believed we didn't need to pinpoint our position. We felt that we were well clear of hazards. When the battery charge was completed, the Captain ordered us to lie-to, secure the engines, and answer bells on the battery. It made me nervous to wallow in this nearly flat calm but I figured that at least I might be able to hear any ships that may have been approaching. They might even be sounding the International Sound signals for ships in fog on the high seas. I would surely have appreciated any ship observing that rule of the road on this night.

The rocking of the ship became more pronounced. Captain Malvern called up to the bridge and ordered the OOD to come around and head into the swell. Mr. Holman gave the appropriate orders. We swung around into the sea and came to all stop. We steadied up for awhile and then:

"Contact bearing 010 degrees!" shouted the starboard lookout.

"I have it in sight," replied Mr. Holman.

"Captain to the bridge!"

We soon saw that the object was a rock. It sent shivers up my spine. If we hit something like that we could have been in serious trouble. When Captain Malvern arrived on the bridge he spotted the object and quickly agreed that it was a large, jagged rock sticking its ugly head out of the water.

"I have the conn, Mr. Holman."

"Aye, Aye, sir. Helm. The Captain has the conn."

"Maneuvering, answer bells on two main engines. All ahead one third, left full rudder."

We left the rock disappearing down our starboard side and took a sounding. We had only 30 feet under our keel. The Captain belatedly ordered the sound heads and Pitt log retracted into the hull. They could have been torn off or smashed if we had grounded or clipped the top of some submerged rock. Twenty minutes or so after the rock disappeared astern into the fog, we were somewhat relieved. I was still quite tense. And justly so. I was worried because we didn't know our exact position and we were obviously near land. We felt a slight shudder and we came to a halt.

"All stop! All back full!"

We had run aground on a sand bar. It was fortunate that the Captain had ordered the sound heads and Pitt log retracted and we going ahead at low speed.. We knew we had to contend with various currents in these waters but the strength of them surprised us.

"All stop! All back full!" the Captain ordered.

"All stop!"

The ship did not move at all.

The Exec was now on the bridge. He suggested to the Captain that we continue to back at one third speed while he had the off-watch crew head back aft. The Captain concurred. He ordered continuous soundings and ordered the SD radar fired up. The ship was sitting on the sand right below the fathometer so it couldn't be used. I thought that it was strange that the Captain would make that kind of mistake.

He seemed edgy tonight.

"All back one third," ordered the Captain.

With the screws turning over slowly at all-back one third, and all available hands aft, the ship assumed a slight up angle and slid easily back off the sand bar. The crew heading aft acted like a reverse negative tank and gave us a down angle while heading astern. It was a technique the German U-Boats used during WWI. Once we were free of the sand bar we came to all stop. The Captain turned the conn over to Mr. Holman again and went below to look at the radar scope. He soon came back to the bridge. He ordered Mr. Holman to come right to course 195 degrees and we headed southeast at one third speed until we were sure that we were out in the main straits. We had to see where we were. The scope had briefly displayed some short blips that could have been near by mountain peaks. That probably showed us we were heading out toward the straits. We had been set down by the current and ran aground on a reef off a small island near the east side of the bay. Fortunately, we were going quite slow and had grounded on a sandy spit off the island and missed some rocks by just a few hundred feet. We were still faced with an unexpectedly strong current. If the fog lifted while we were grounded so near to the populated islands we'd have been dead ducks.

At day break the Japanese couldn't have missed us. Once we regained our orientation we headed farther into the straights at full speed. Never a dull moment on this patrol so far. It seemed Murphy's Law was working over time. "If anything can go wrong, it will, and at the worse possible time."

The grounding episode had unnerved me to the extent that when I got off watch I was too agitated to sleep. I got my writing gear from under my bunk and headed into the Crew's Mess. I sat down and started to write another letter to Meilin. This time I told her a little bit more about my childhood. She was very interested in my background and the area where I was raised. It seemed that every time we had some kind of emergency aboard the *Dolphin* it would help calm me down when I started putting words to her on paper. She was beginning to become important to me.

The next morning the fog had dissipated and we were able to check our position by the landmarks we knew so well by now. We prepared to submerge. The weather was clear and calm. With the fog gone, the Captain decided to try the easternmost channel again. He knew it would give us a broader view of the upper reaches of the bay. The eastern channel, again proved to be too narrow and too shallow. We had to maneuver through a multitude of sampans and fishing nets with their glass floats. You'd think that we should have learned that lesson. After a few hours of that, we headed back out to the straits. The Captain decided our best bet would be the channel in the western side of the bay. It was in the lee of the mountains and we wouldn't have to contend with the steady chop created by the wind in the eastern channel. Also, the western channel appeared free of fishing boats. I wondered why. Maybe the fishing was better in the eastern channel.   That evening as we charged batteries and performed the usual routine, we could see at least two light houses. These Japanese lighthouses were well placed and gave us good bearings.

There was just a sliver of a moon, and a mist was forming. Captain Malvern decided we should make good a track between two points of land and reverse course when a certain bearing of each point was reached. He had written those instructions in the night order book, That way we could keep aware of how the current was setting us. As we plodded along at one third speed on one main engine, the mist had become a thick fog and hid the main deck from the bridge. Eerily, the top of the periscope shears started to glow with white luminescence. It covered the radio masts and the A-frames as well as the bridge and was slowly dropping. It was spooky.

Mr. Molloy, who was the OOD, said, "It looks like old Saint Elmo is paying us a visit."

"What do you mean?" I asked.

"Haven't you heard of St. Elmo's fire?"

"No, sir, I haven't."

"It's got something to do with an electrical charge of some sort. In the days of the early sailing ships, a ball of glowing electrical energy usually appeared somewhere in the rigging. If it was seen to rise, the sailors considered it a good omen. If it dropped toward the deck it portended bad luck for the ship. Shining on the face of a sailor meant ill fortune for him. "

"Who was St. Elmo?"

"I don't recall, but he is regarded as the patron saint of sailors or by those who make their living on the sea."

The bridge watch was now all ears at Mr. Molloy's tale. I can't blame them since there was not much to see with their binoculars. It made for a fascinating story.

"I don't believe all that stuff," said Porky.

All of us on the bridge looked at each other. Our faces were now being lit up as if by a ceiling light. All of us wondered about the veracity of his story. Especially since this glow gradually dropped *from top to bottom*. I wondered then if this new omen would cancel out the omen I experienced the first evening we were at sea on this trip. The flash of blue-green light.

The next morning we submerged and crept into the bay on the western side. The Captain raising the scope periodically and looking around. Depth control soon became a problem in this channel. Our neutral buoyancy and fore and aft trim was computed based on the salt water out in the straits. In the channel we were in increasingly dense fresh water from the streams cascading down the mountain sides. The rain and melting snow on the mountain tops provided copious quantities of fresh water sliding under the salt water. Fresh water is not as buoyant as salt water and we would sometimes sink below periscope depth and have to plane up by adding speed.

One time we hit a pocket of salt water between a couple of patches of fresh water and shot up like a balloon. We broached; a cardinal sin for submarines. Once you dive you are not supposed to expose any part of the submarine with the exception of the tips of the periscopes. We increased our speed fast enough to drive us under in a hurry. Lt. Bob Molloy, our diving officer and engineer, did a masterful job of maintaining periscope depth all the while complaining about the noisy trim pump. The pistons clattered and we were glad that we weren't being hunted by destroyers. Clyde said there was nothing that could be done to quiet the trim pump. We sorely needed a more powerful and quieter one. We had heard the newer boats had deep-well turbine bowls set in parallel that did a terrific job of quickly and quietly moving the tons of water that were needed to adjust the trim. They were not a source of noise as the piston powered pumps were.

We headed into the bay and we could see, through the periscope, the Japanese houses to the west nestled on the hillsides and the roads running past them. You can see how close to shore we were. This channel was deeper and allowed us to get farther into the bay. On one observation the Captain saw an airplane heading out over the bay and he ordered 120 feet and right full rudder, reversing course. As we turned, the skipper took a good look up the channel.
"I see some cranes or derricks. It looks like there might a shipyard. Possibly a Naval base. Down scope."
If that were true it could explain the reason for the scarcity of fishing boats. Naval traffic might be keeping them out of the channel. Maybe the Japanese navy had some regulation that commercial fishing boats were warned about.
That night we surfaced in the wide mouth of the bay for battery charging and trash dumping. The breeze in the balmy atmosphere carried the aroma of the Japanese country side. It was different and yet very pleasant. One could imagine the Japanese families cooking and eating around their little hibachis. None of us had ever been to Japan except for the Exec. Mr. Bass who had lived in Yokohama for three years when his father, also a Naval Academy graduate, was serving as Naval Attaché at the United States Embassy in Tokyo.
Japanese were a very mysterious people to most of us. Having lived on the west coast of California for most of my life, I attended school with some Japanese kids; they were private and didn't socialize at all with Caucasians. In the movie thrillers during the period before World War II, orientals were portrayed as mysterious and sinister. They were always the villains. The one exception to that portrayal was Earl der Bigger's Charlie Chan, the detective. He was supposed to be Chinese; although we knew even less about the

Chinese. Chan was played in the movies by either Warner Oland or Sid Toler, both Caucasians, which demonstrates how little we knew about Orientals. I was fortunate to have had ties with a group of Chinese kids that attended school with me in San Francisco. I was the only Caucasian on a Chinese basketball team. I came to know the Chinese people a little better than most of my shipmates. My relationship with Meilin and her family increased my understanding of Orientals much more.

Lying-to and charging batteries, we relaxed and perhaps dropped our guard. This had become so routine to us. Suddenly one of the look-outs spotted a ship coming out of the main channel. It had its running lights on. We could see its starboard green running light. The ship turned toward us as we watched. Both the port and starboard lights became clearly visible. The OOD pulled the plug and under we went. We were rapidly approaching 120 feet when the crunching cement mixer noise of twin screws passed directly overhead. The contact noise soon faded away. After an hour's wait we surfaced and proceeded farther out into the straits again with two direct engines on propulsion while we continued to charge batteries on the two diesel electric engines. In the control room Mr. Bass said to no one in particular:

"I wonder if this activity is what we are supposed to be looking for?"

Captain Malvern who had come into the compartment added:

"Perhaps this is a clue for us. We'll really have to keep on our toes from now on."

Heading in to the bay the next morning, we spotted a small ship that looked like one of our World War I sub chasers. It seemed to be just puttering around in the area where we submerged with no apparent purpose. It wasn't going anywhere. We eased by it at 100 feet and continued up the westernmost channel, this time heading closer to the western side. We were surprised by the sonar operator reporting he had picked up sounds of a ship coming up the channel behind us. The Captain ordered 125 feet. We had never yet seen a ship enter this channel. Captain Malvern was, as usual, nervous. We kept silent and listened to the contact as it passed over us into the harbor. The sonar operator in the forward torpedo room reported:

"Conn, Sonar. The contact appears to have twin screws. Probably a destroyer."

"Sonar, Conn. Very well"

The propeller noise faded as we came back up to periscope depth. The Captain reversed course and headed back out the channel. Just then sonar picked up more screw noise.

"Conn, Sonar. More screw noise dead astern in the channel."

The Captain ordered periscope depth and raised the scope, looked up channel and found that there were at least two destroyers heading toward us down the channel toward the straits. The Captain again ordered 125 feet. The sudden ship activity seemed to confirm the Naval base theory. In this relatively narrow channel it became apparent that the destroyers would pass over us. We continued heading out toward the straits. Proceeding at the slowest speed we could and still maintaining depth control, *Dolphin* plodded out to deep water. We didn't dare turn on our fathometer, knowing that the sound would likely alert the destroyers overhead. We were in an awkward position. The Exec told me since we were in Japanese waters and not in international waters we could be construed as pirates under international law. If we were detected and caught we could be executed without a trial. It would place the United States in an embarrassing position in the world community. I didn't relish the thought of the possibility of being executed if we were caught.

It seemed an eternity before we reached the mouth of the bay but the Captain, being extra cautious, wanted to stay submerged for another hour. He also wanted to get out of the shipping channel. We had been submerged for twelve hours. It was the first time since I reported aboard that we had been down for more than eight hours in one day.

When we finally surfaced that night, Porky, one of the look-outs who was aptly named because he was quite round around his belt line, asked, "The air smells funny. Are we were near land or something?"

"What you smell, young man, is fresh air," said the Captain.

Porky shrugged his shoulders and raised his binoculars to his eyes again. It showed that you could easily get used to the foul air below decks.

The garbage and sanitary tank routine was implemented and a battery charge started. Lying-to with the engines cramming juice into the batteries, the starboard lookout spotted a contact coming out of the western channel as it did the night before. It turned toward us again and seemed to pick up speed. We submerged and eased under. The noise stopped. Why had the ship stopped?. Had it seen us? We went to silent running just in case, and put our stern toward the contact. The noise soon started up again and then faded away. The captain decided to stay down at 125 feet for another two hours. The air got stifling. We needed to surface.

The next morning we approached the western channel this time venturing farther up the bay. A strong onshore wind created a sizeable chop on the surface of the water which helped conceal our periscope observations. We could leave the scope up a little longer without worrying about leaving a telltale feather of a wake trailing behind. On one observation, Captain Malvern, a normally soft-spoken man, shouted:

"*High level bombers heading over the bay! Down scope!* Those planes must have come off the carrier we saw launching aircraft out in the straits."

"Up scope! Put me on the last bearing…there…that's it. *It looks like they're dropping bombs.*"

Captain Malvern took one full fast sweep with the scope and ordered, "Down scope! Reverse course and let's get out of here. Mark your depth!"

"Five, five feet. At ordered depth, sir," answered the diving officer.

"Very well. Make your depth 100 feet. All ahead two thirds."

Mr. Bass suggested that if they were dropping bombs we should be able to hear or at least feel the vibrations from the explosions. There were no explosions.

"Very strange!. Why aren't the bombs exploding? What's going on?" asked the Exec.

"They were dropping something that sure looked like bombs to me."

The Captain, fearing that we might be seen by aircraft in such shallow water, ordered 125 feet and headed out into the straits for deeper water. We surfaced and started our surfacing routine including a battery charge.

Later that night we saw the running lights of a ship coming out the channel. Again it turned toward us. We submerged. It passed over us but didn't stop this time. Surfacing an hour later, the Captain ordered us to head farther out in the straits to complete our battery charge. It was too late and too dark to take any star sights. I didn't think they were necessary anyway considering what we were doing. We had a lot of landmarks we could rely on by now.

We submerged earlier the next morning and headed back in. As we entered the mouth of the bay again, the Captain observed a bunch of small craft converging where we had been forced under the night before. I wondered what they were doing. Were they fishing boats or could they be naval auxiliaries? They didn't seem to pose any threat to us, so we proceeded submerged well beneath them. This time Captain Malvern took us farther up the western channel. On one periscope observation he slammed the scope handles up and yelled:

"Down scope!"

The Captain looked pale. Sweat poured down his face. Something had gotten to him.

"Torpedo bombers, lots of 'em, flying low and dropping torpedoes! I've got to take another look. Up scope."

He steadied the scope and held it on one bearing for about twenty seconds. Thank God, we had that heavy chop and were at dead slow.

"Down scope. Lots of buoys with pennants on them and several markers along the shoreline. It looks like a simulation of some sort. Let's get the hell out of here. Left full rudder!"

Captain Malvern ordered 125 feet. It was a blessing that we had such a deep channel. We reversed course and began our slow return to the straits. That was the first time since Captain Malvern assumed command that he used the word "hell". Our previous skipper used plenty of foul language when things didn't go right. The Exec and I both noted that there were no explosions this time either.

"Captain, there were no explosions today; just like yesterday. You also mentioned that it looked like a simulation of some sort. What do you think is happening?"

"I don't know, Mr. Bass, but it sure doesn't look like any amphibious landing exercise that we're supposed to be checking out. Maybe it is some kind of Japanese Navy-Day celebration and they are putting on a demonstration for the local citizenry."

That bothered me, too. If this had been in the Atlantic I would have immediately assumed that it was a dress rehearsal for some major operation. The Germans had been known to do dry runs on certain elaborate operations. But here in the Pacific... I didn't know. A new assault on China? Maybe? The Japanese were rattling their sabers all over the Far East. We didn't know what to make of the scene the Captain was viewing. He was the eyes of the ship.

It was about 2100 that night when we surfaced. The moon had set and it was dark with only the stars blinking. Down below in the control room:

"I would like to get a radar image if we can."

"We can't, Captain. The SD is only able to detect aircraft up to 15 miles or so."

"We could use a radar like our destroyers have. It would be extremely valuable in cases like this."

At about 0230 in the morning the starboard lookout called, *"Contact bearing zero one zero."*

"Mr. Holman, I have him in sight too. No running lights."

I was on the bridge at the time and looked toward that bearing. I saw a streak of phosphorescence about 8,000 yards off. In waters that teemed with plankton, large fish such as porpoises would stir up the water causing the organisms to become phosphorescent. Ships would have the same effect. In this case it was a ship and this time there were no running lights visible.

The OOD also saw the streak of phosphorescence and he sounded the diving klaxon twice yelling, *"Clear the bridge, Clear the bridge! Dive, Dive!"*

The five of us scrambled to get below. The two lookouts, the helmsman, myself, and Mr. Holman. As we were passing through periscope depth Captain Malvern, who had come into the control room, ordered 175 feet and silent running. We shut down everything that was not absolutely needed to run the ship.

We went deeper than we had before and when we reached 175 feet we were heading farther out toward the straits. Had we been detected? It sure seemed like it to me. There was total silence in both the control room and the conning tower as we anxiously listened. You could hear the clock ticking and the occasional, slight squeaking noise that told us the planes were being operated. Sonar reported they appeared to have changed their course and were proceeding in a direction away from us. Apparently they lost contact with us. Thank God!

You could tell the tension was high. Mr. Holman had large sweat rings under both arms and both the bow and stern planes operators had streaks of sweat running down the backs of their blue dungaree shirts. They hadn't done enough physical effort to warrant that much perspiration. I didn't think to look at myself but I'm sure that I offered the same kind of display.

We took our time and crept back up to 125 feet where we spent about an hour listening. We headed on several different courses in order to ensure that we had scoured the area by sonar and hadn't missed a sleeping enemy. The JK sonar, with its crystals, was so good that at times we could hear the oars of a rowboat splashing or a small boat under sail. We could occasionally hear a rain squall. Finally back at periscope depth it looked clear and after a couple of prolonged looks, we surfaced. It was black out with no moon and with a cloud cover that cut off whatever starlight there might have been. We couldn't see any ships. The captain ordered the battery charge resumed and we started to calm down somewhat.

We had been on the surface about an hour and my blood pressure felt like it had dropped back to normal when suddenly our ship was surrounded by bright light reflecting off of the water. The short hair of my crew cut stood straight up. We discovered that the light came from our contour lights.

"Control, Bridge. Turn off the contour lights. Now!" shouted the OOD.

"Bridge, Control. They're off. Sorry about that, sir."

The 7MC was a fast way to get a message below. On the bridge we were temporarily blinded by the lights and approaching ships would not be visible to us. It took us at least thirty minutes to become partially dark adapted again. It was an hour before we were totally dark adapted. In peace time, three to four lights were installed on each side of the submarine's superstructure, to provide an outline of the ship's contour while at anchor in a harbor as a measure to prevent accidental ramming at night. A submarine at anchor with its low silhouette could easily be mistaken for a small fishing boat and if it were accidentally rammed its low margin of positive buoyancy would vanish and the ship would sink. The submarine had to be outlined for any passing ships to be able to see that it was larger than it looked, especially on a moonless night. We found out that the electrician who turned on the lights assumed he was turning on an interior lighting circuit. The fuses were pulled to avoid another such incident. It took us a good hour before our night vision was back to normal.

The Captain came to the bridge and said he didn't think that the Japanese could have seen the light as far out as we were. I sure hoped so but he wasn't on the bridge when the lights were on.. At the thought that the Japanese might possibly have seen us I became even more nervous if that was possible. We stayed on the surface but it was an uneasy watch for me the rest of that night.

Chapter VI: Give Us This Day

Mr. Holman and Ding-Dong had just settled down into the four to eight watch on the bridge when the 7MC sounded:
"Conn. Sonar. I have high speed screws approaching off of our port beam."
Sure enough. In the murky pre-dawn atmosphere there was the telltale phosphorescence in the water indicating a ship heading directly towards us. It had no running lights showing this time and was about 4500 yards away. We made a quick dive and headed deep.
The Captain who was in the control room ordered, "Make your depth 200 feet and come to course 195 degrees."
The planesmen and the helmsman under Mr. Holman's direction, as diving officer now, complied with those orders. I wondered why the Captain ordered 200 feet instead of the usual 120 or 125 feet. Did he know something? The hull started to creak and groan as we got deeper. There were several different sounds that we normally didn't hear. It was simply the ship adjusting to the increased pressure as we went deeper.
The Captain ordered, "Come left to course 185 degrees. All ahead one third."
He was turning away from the contact to present our screws toward him and give him the narrowest contact we could. Any sound he might hear would be mushy and indistinct because of the wash from our screws. As we were passing through 100 feet we were hit with a sharp high pitched squeal. The ship, now obviously a destroyer, had started echo-ranging. Pinging! What a shock! I noticed Mr. Bass and the Captain exchanging startled looks. The

United States Navy was aware that the Japanese destroyers had sonar and knew they could listen but didn't know they could echo-range as well. Our Navy still considered that the Japanese had a very primitive navy. The Navy had obviously forgotten what the Japanese navy did to the Russian fleet at the turn of the century in the battle of Tsu-Shima in 1904. The Japanese soundly defeated the Russians. They also had raided Vladivostok in a manner similar to their raid on Pearl Harbor only with torpedo boats instead of airplanes.

What an eerie feeling to clearly hear those high pitched squeals directly through the hull. Echo-ranging sends an electrical impulse through the water and when it hits a solid object such as the hull of a submarine the impulse bounces back to the sender as an echo slightly diminished. The time it takes the pulse to travel to the target and return can easily be computed into range. Submerged reefs and underwater mountain tops can be detected on the same principle. The Japanese obviously knew that they had something out there and they were trying to find it. I wondered if they had seen the bright luminescent glow of our contour lights that were inadvertently switched on the night before.

Passing over us the Japanese ship turned and headed back towards us. They shifted to short scale pinging, a more rapid pulsing. Which meant by U.S. Navy standards, they were sure they had a contact. Normal pinging simply means the surface ship is searching and when they get an echo they turn to more rapid pinging to pinpoint the target more closely. I knew then that they had detected us. My thoughts were glum. Would they try to sink us or perhaps try to force us to surface?

We could tell from Sonar that this ship was heading directly toward us again. The Captain ordered right full rudder and went to all ahead dead slow. The ship passed overhead at a high rate of speed. The destroyer's screws sounded like a handful of pea-gravel being shaken up in a tin can. Sonar reported splashes on the surface from the JK. A few seconds later: blam, blam, blam, blam!

Four terrific and very loud explosions. They were dropping depth charges. Only a few of us had heard a depth charge before. Most of

TOP SECRET

us had been aboard one day when they dropped some small charges, about the size of hand grenades, 2,000 yards off outside of Pearl Harbor. They called it depth charge indoctrination. Let me tell you that it in no way prepared us for this!

Today when movies depict a depth charging scene they show everyone screaming and a lot of noise. In reality those situations were faced with hardly a voice being raised. Everyone would be at their battle station and knew what they had to do. There was no need to shout and usually not even necessary to talk. During, this, our first depth charging everyone reacted in the way they were trained. The exec recommended to the Captain that we man battle stations - torpedo and put the smoking lamp out. The Captain, who's knuckle's were white from gripping the edge of the table over the master gyro, said nothing. He just nodded his agreement.

The Japanese came back again and dropped four more accurately placed depth charges. At that moment both ICMG's (the interior communications motor generators) chose to kick out. Our lighting, fire control and communication circuits were lost. We had to grope in the dark to find and turn on our emergency battle lanterns for light. One of those lanterns was flung off of the bulkhead by the force of the explosion and it's light had turned on. It made me acutely aware of the force of the explosions because the lantern weighed about five pounds. Those lanterns didn't come on automatically as they did in the latter stages of WW II and when the lights go out aboard a submerged submarine it is totally black inside. There is no ambient light. A few of the clocks had phosphorescent hands and numbers on them but they faded quickly. The auxiliary electrician pushed the breakers back in, restarted the motor generators and adjusted the rheostats to divide the load equally between the two. Power and lights were soon restored. Later submarines had four ICMG's but balancing the load between them still became a problem at times. One of the generators would try to hog the load but when it got the load it couldn't hold it alone and dropped it. Everything went black again.

The wash from the depth charges subsided but the noise

continued to roar. It didn't have the impact noise of a depth charge but it was almost as loud and lasted for about fifteen minutes.

The Exec yelled, "Oh shit. One or two, maybe all three of the torpedoes in the deck storage lockers are running hot."

"If we can go deeper maybe the water pressure will shut them down."

"Mr. Holman, it will only slow them down a bit. We can't do anything about it. We have to let them use up their fuel. They're letting a lot of noise and steam into the water. Our only hope is that the Japs continue pinging and not listening. We're letting a lot of bubbles out in the water as well."

When the Mark 14 torpedoes that we carried were fired the flash boilers they contained would almost immediately start producing steam and driving the torpedo's propellers. The steam and smoke from the burning alcohol would be released through the torpedoes after body leaving a trail of bubbles through the water which could lead an enemy to their source. In this case, the *Dolphin*. One or more of the torpedoes had started to run hot in the deck locker. Having no place to go and since it was confined and not fired, would simply generate steam and smoke. The bubbles would float to the surface as was normal. The shock from the depth charge explosion apparently set the torpedoes engines off. It made an unusually loud racket because the fish was confined in a steel deck locker and the noise was amplified.

We were sweating it out trying to maintain 200 feet.

Suddenly Porky, who was operating the stern planes called out, "Sir! The stern planes are not working! Permission to shift to hand power."

"Shift the stern planes to hand power!"

Mr. Molloy, who had assumed the diving officer responsibility at battle stations, watched as Porky switched the power selector to hand power in an attempt to operate the stern planes. Porky flipped the control lever to manual and extended the retractable handle on the thirty inch in diameter wheel which gave him the leverage to turn the hydraulic pump by hand. That would force the hydraulic oil through the lines to operate the planes.

"They're still not working, sir!"

"Get some one on the stern planes hydraulic system, now!" shouted Mr. Molloy.

What a time for the stern planes to crap out. Clyde started to check out the system and found that the IMO pump and its electric motor were fine. There had to be a break in the hydraulic lines somewhere between the control room and the after torpedo room. He headed aft looking for the answer. Clyde came back with a report he tersely delivered as he disappeared down the pump room hatch. The electrolysis between the copper piping and the steel bracket holding it in place had caused the pipe to erode almost completely through. The shock of the depth charging finished the job by breaking the pipe thus filling the after torpedo room bilges with hydraulic oil. The unseen devils that were causing our electrolysis and corrosion problems had taken this occasion, with the help of the depth charging, to brandish their power over us.

Clyde, climbing up out of the pump room, briefly told us that he could probably sweat a sleeve over the leaking portion of the hydraulic line and secure it to the stanchion. He added that he hoped we had enough hydraulic oil aboard to refill that part of the system. Clyde went back to the after torpedo room with an acetylene torch and tank. He immediately started to take care of that "little" problem. I didn't think of it at the time but using a torch would have burned up a lot of good oxygen. Things didn't look good for the *Dolphin* at this point in the game, if you could call this situation a game.

Mr. Molloy at first had no problem maintaining depth without having control of the stern planes. Then he needed rise on the stern planes. His options were to pump from the after trim tank to sea or to put some air in number seven main ballast tank. Air was precious and difficult to control. The trim pump was noisy but could do the job. Since the trim adjustment was minor, Mr. Molloy opted to use the trim pump. A brief clattering and the required number of pounds of water were pumped out to sea. Depth charges started raining down on us. The Japs had definitely heard the trim pump clattering. They were listening as well as pinging. We were now acutely aware of how noisy the trim pump was. We hadn't given it much thought before.

No United States Navy submarine, that I know of, had ever experienced a depth charge attack before. It was frightening. Most, if not all, of us were scared stiff. I thought the end was near. Mr. Bass said he wondered how the guys back aft were making out. So did I. He took a quick trip through the boat to check on conditions and the reactions of the crew. When he came back to the control room he told us that the crew was holding up quite well, especially those in the maneuvering spaces who were busy operating the levers to adjust the ship's speed as they received orders from control. He said that he saw lots of pale faces and perspiration rings on their dungaree shirts. All hands were essentially okay. Mostly scared, but okay.

Two more Japanese destroyers had joined up with the first one. They were churning up the surface with all the power they could muster. They would head away from us, as near as we could tell, and then come right back over one after the other and accurately drop more depth charges. It appeared these destroyers were no amateurs in their job of ASW (anti-submarine warfare).

Tension was high in the control room and I knew the rest of the crew in the other compartments were as nervous and apprehensive as we were. A report came in from the engine room that the last series of depth charges had lifted the engine room hatch allowing a shower of cold salt water into the compartment. Sea pressure quickly resealed the hatch. It was similar to an earthquake when something is momentarily distorted and then resumes its shape. At the same moment a 500 pound air line supplying the starting pressure for the diesel engines busted loose. The line whipped as it broke and hit Johnson on the forearm. He was later diagnosed as having one of the bones broken and the Doc had to put a splint on it. The motor machinists shut a stop valve saving precious air. Mr. Molloy attempting to keep our stern toward our attackers was using very little speed. The Captain said nothing. He looked pale. All the rest of us must have appeared the same.

Trying to ease our tensions, Mr. Bass told us the depth charges were merely irritants. He said that if we were at war we could employ a technique he learned at his Tactics class. We could plane up to 120 feet and fire two circular running torpedoes; one to port and one to starboard followed by two more in the same fashion and maybe two more after that. Four to six steam torpedoes running and leaving a wake in a 1200 yard radius circle at about a five to ten foot depth would obviously make it exceedingly dangerous for any surface ship to cross through that pattern to drop depth charges. However, in this case there was still a remote chance the Japanese weren't sure they had a submarine contact. If we had fired only one torpedo it would have been a dead give away.

    Chief Brown suggested that we load some debris in a torpedo tube and blow it out to convince the Japs that they had sunk a submarine. We would have had to withdraw a torpedo from one of the tubes before we could do that and it would take a lot of time. The Exec said that we would again be confirming to the Japanese that they definitely had a submarine contact and we didn't want to do that. Mr. Bass added that the debris would probably identify us positively as a U.S. submarine. He was sure right on that score and the idea was promptly dropped. The torpedo men didn't like the idea of fouling up their tubes with junk either. But I was sure the Japs knew they had forced a foreign submarine down; they just didn't know from what country's navy.

    I was in the conning tower as we eased up to 125 feet and listened. Everything unessential was shut down and secured. Sonar reported there were two sets of screws off of our port bow and they were coming toward us fast. Captain Malvern again ordered 200 feet. Several more depth charges were dropped, doing little more than to shake us up a bit this time. Sonar reported that the destroyers had continued on and hadn't turned back to make another attack. The Captain ordered periscope depth; 62 feet.

    When we slowed down enough for the Captain to use the scope he ordered, "Up periscope".

    As I pressed the periscope control I received a jolt of electricity. Salt water was starting to ground out the control. The scope's packing glands were leaking like sieves giving Captain Malvern a good shower. He took a long look all around. Sonar reported that he couldn't hear any screw noises. Captain Malvern said it was clear but completely overcast. He said he didn't see any destroyers or other ships in the area.

We had been submerged for over ten hours and the battery was getting low, so Captain Malvern ordered us to surface. We had no sooner reached the bridge when sonar called up saying that there were high speed propellers close aboard off the port bow and coming in fast. The Captain immediately ordered a quick dive and as the quartermaster of the watch I quickly shut the hatch. The engines hadn't even had enough time to even get started. Captain Malvern then ordered:

"Left full rudder! All ahead flank! Make your depth 200 feet. I intend to swing toward and under him."

I'm sure he was hoping we could get deep enough fast enough to cause the Japs to overshoot with their depth charges. I thought the fast changing relative bearing rate would cause the destroyer to possibly lose contact and he might not drop any charges. Four more close depth charges blew that theory all to hell. The hand wheel of a small valve was spun so hard by the blast it came off its stem and smacked me in the face. I had a fat lip for a few days. Later I lost three front teeth from abscesses that developed as a result of that encounter. A motor machinist in the engine room was knocked off his feet and cut his arm on something as he fell. He also got a gash on his forehead. In the forward torpedo room a torpedo man who was stepping in to the compartment as one of the charges went off suffered a sprained ankle. It was a wonder he didn't break it.

We had been the victim of a sleeper. The first two destroyers had proceeded noisily on a constant course away from us while a third was lying-to, listening. Visibility from periscope depth is limited and the Jap was lying outside that distance but near enough to hear us and catch us by surprise. What saved us from being rammed was the fact that it took a little time for the destroyer to get up to speed from being dead in the water while listening. This type of anti-submarine strategy by the Japanese was to be observed frequently during the ensuing war.

Captain Malvern then ordered us to level out at 200 feet. The ship creaked and groaned all the way down. I wondered if the Japanese could hear all that noise as clearly as we could. The Japanese had to be aware of our presence by now. But how did they find out? Had they seen our contour lights we accidentally turned on the other night? We thought we had been careful and those lights were on for only a short period of time. Perhaps as little as one minute. That question will probably never be answered.

Still in the mouth of the bay, the Captain headed us out to deeper water turning our stern toward our attacker. We continued to proceed farther out into the straits. We were at dead slow and had shut down every piece of equipment we didn't absolutely need. The Japs came back again and dropped four more depth charges. This time very close aboard. but still above us, thank God. Sonar reported the last attack had apparently shattered the JK crystals in that side of the sonar head but he could still listen with the QC on the other side. The rods and cones had held up fine under the blasts. We had lost our very fine listening ability when we lost the JK.

The ship, normally quite stable while submerged, shook and rocked violently with each depth charge attack. Some of the crew were knocked off the benches or stools they were sitting on and those who were standing had to be holding on to something or else they would have been thrown to the deck. The noise was deafening. A few of us felt as if the hull was going to collapse and we'd be finished. I noticed that whenever the charges went off nearly directly overhead the depth gauges showed that we were pushed downward about twenty feet or so. It was scary. Going deeper by intent was one thing but being pushed down by an explosion was still another.

The Captain who had been looking at the chart, ordered, *"Make your depth 400 feet!"*

Our test depth! Various packing glands were leaking and in some cases salt water was spurting from them. Many of the crew were busy tightening valve packing glands which were leaking in every compartment. Sully, who had come forward for a cup of coffee, came into the control room. He whispered to me that the packing around the propeller shafts was starting to ooze out into the motor room. He headed back aft to the engine room with his cup of coffee. How he could even think about coffee during this calamity was beyond my feeble comprehension.

The Captain ordered us to put *Dolphin* on the bottom. We had never done that since I was aboard her. As far as I knew, no one else aboard had ever been aboard a submarine that had deliberately bottomed before. It was 400 to 450 feet deep here, well below our test depth. We knew from our charts there was a sand and mud bottom but there were also many large rocks on either side of the channel.

As we passed through about 375 feet there was an extremely loud explosion that came from just aft of the bridge. We could not figure out what it was but it apparently did not cause any more leaks. It took some time to figure out that it was the implosion of our small boat container which was on deck just aft of the conning tower and above the deck torpedo stowage. It probably let out a large air bubble followed by an oil slick and maybe a small oil and gas can or two. Maybe even the small boat itself or pieces of it. The boat was sixteen feet long and of wooden construction. Hopefully all the debris was contained within the collapsed container, but at least it surely leaked some additional oil if not a chunk of wood or two.

Mr. Molloy who was battle stations diving officer ordered, "All stop. Pass the word to the forward room to retract the pit log and sound heads into the hull."

He did that so they wouldn't be damaged when we hit bottom. He then ordered, "All ahead dead slow."

Lt. Molloy needed headway to keep control of our direction and trim. It took a concentrated effort on his part to set us down gently and evenly. He flooded a few hundred pounds of water into the auxiliary tanks but depended a lot on the compression of the hull as we got deeper to increase our negative buoyancy. It was tense in the control room while watching the needles on the depth gauges drop so slowly. It seemed like an eternity as we gradually settled down. All of us had our fingers crossed, hoping that we wouldn't hit any of the rocks. I glanced around the control room and wondered if any of the other guys had visions, as I had, of a large rock suddenly poking its sharp point up through the hull. Lt. Molloy had flooded just enough sea water to the auxiliary tanks to give us a slight negative buoyancy enabling us to land slowly and softly.

Just seconds before we hit he had ordered, "All Stop."

When we hit, all of us in the control room breathed a sigh of relief. Our relief was tangible as we kind of settled into the mud and sand as opposed to hitting bottom with a sharp impact. Mr. Molloy completely flooded negative and all auxiliary and trim tanks to give us as much extra weight as he could to hold us down. Even with all that we still rocked in the current. Had we not been in such a precarious position it would have seemed like a gigantic hand rocking a huge cradle.. The current hardly moved us. Just a slight swaying. It was hard for me to believe I had been so tense waiting for the *Dolphin* to hit bottom especially since it was below our "not to exceed" test depth. I suddenly became aware of my feelings and I started to relax a little. I shivered a bit.

The Japs came over again and dropped another four depth charges but they were not nearly as close as the first ones and they were considerably astern of us. The depth charges were apparently set above 175 feet. The explosions weren't so loud and the *Dolphin* wasn't reeling and pitching any more. Were we getting used to depth charges? I wasn't and I'm sure the rest of the crew felt the same way. The *Dolphin* lay still as we tried to consolidate our thoughts and evaluate our situation. In minutes the destroyers were coming back and another four depth charges were dropped followed quickly by four more. Again those "ash-cans" came close but not so close as the first ones. It was still frightening. I thought the bulkheads were going to collapse.

There was a lull in the activity of the destroyers on the surface. The depth charging stopped. I commented that maybe the destroyers had to return to port to load up with more charges. Mr. Bass ordered all hands to rest easy at battle stations. With the sound gear retracted into the hull we couldn't hear much of what was happening on the surface. We didn't have the deck mounted sonar that the newer boats had. That would have been helpful to us now.

The Captain called a conference of all the officers in the ward room. He had the Chief-of-the-Boat, the ET, Brad French, and me (as the senior Quartermaster) included in the meeting. The first thing he asked how we thought the Japs found out we were there. Chief Brown said they might have noticed the damage we did to their fishing nets. I ventured they could have spotted some of our trash floating and noticed that it was not from the Japanese fishing boats. Mr. Holman added that the Sub Chaser type vessel we saw puttering around might have been picking up our trash and garbage. Brad pointed out that the radar antenna, originally intended for radio, was omni-directional and they could maybe home in on it. I added that our contour lights might have been seen. Mr. Bass said while he lived in Japan he noticed the Japanese appeared to have excellent vision and not at all like the stereotypes in the movies of that period showed them wearing thick eye glasses. The Exec added that they could have been excellent lookouts aboard ship. He said the Japanese very likely had excellent optical equipment as well.

Lt. Molloy, the engineer, came late to the meeting. He reported he'd inspected all compartments and there were no major flooding problems. A few of the *Dolphin's* compartments, most of them aft, had reported minor leaks and some damage. He thought we likely had many rivets in our fuel oil ballast tanks that had been sprung or been tweaked and we were probably leaking a lot of diesel oil. Captain Malvern closed the meeting by saying we would stay down for another couple of hours. Mr. Bass asked permission to order the crew to stand easy at battle stations. The Captain nodded his OK. Mr. Bass had forgotten he had already passed that word.

A few hours went by. The Captain came to the control room. He was pale and appeared agitated. His eyes were darting around the compartment and his normally cold, steely look had changed to a wide-eyed, empty stare. He said nothing. Mr. Bass brought the Captain up to date on the status of the leaks and damage assessment.

The Captain did not acknowledge what Mr. Bass had said.. He didn't even nod. I thought the strain was getting to him. It was getting to me too and I didn't have any responsibilities compared to what he had. At length, Captain Malvern asked the Exec which way the current flowed in the straits. East to west he was told. That might explain why the later depth charges were not close. The current apparently was moving the diesel oil well away from us. The Captain then ordered Lt. Molloy to get us off the bottom and make his depth 70 feet. I wondered what was going on. I figured the *old man* probably wanted to move farther out in the straits where the leaking oil would be carried away faster and cause the Japanese to lose contact. But why take us up to periscope depth? We needed to get farther away and try to lose our tormentors.

After rounds of noisy pumping and blowing, we sluggishly rocked back and forth and finally pulled loose from the suction of the mud and the sand bottom. As soon as he could lower the sound head, Sonar searched all around and reported the area appeared to be all clear of all ships. Easing around with left 15 degrees rudder we headed south east into the current and toward deeper water. An hour later we were well out of the bay but still in its wide mouth when the Captain ordered periscope depth. We rose slowly and when we reached 62 feet.

The Captain ordered, "'Up Scope." He took a swing around and shouted, "Take her deep! All ahead full! I see a destroyer. There's another one coming out the channel. Make your depth 400 feet."

We headed toward the bottom and, after retracting the sound head, hit; this time not so gently. The Japanese were well aware that they had a submarine beneath them and after another short pinging session on us they dropped a batch of four to eight charges. We were lucky. Thankfully they were still not very close. It appeared, as I had thought, they had indeed gone back into port to reload. We were shook up by those explosions again. By my count we had at least five destroyers that were now pummeling us. The noise from their depth charges started up again and seemed to be continuous. The charges started to taper off and then ceased altogether.

Early the next morning we heard the deep rumble of screws from the direction of the east channel. It sounded like a large, slow freighter and apparently had only a single screw. The noise gave me an ominous feeling. I had the same feeling of a cloud blocking out the sun as I felt the last day at the beach. As we listened we heard what sounded like an anchor being lowered. We heard the slow thump, thump of a ships propellers approaching. It was accompanied by eerie vibrating sounds, humming like a strong wind blowing across telephone lines. The sounds came closer. There was something being dragged through the water toward us. The screw noises grew louder and louder. We heard all these sounds directly through the hull. Our sonar gear had been retracted into the hull.

The whirring sound seemed to pass down our port side and fade a bit. Then the vibrating whine appeared to pass down our starboard side in the opposite direction. It was obvious that they were making passes with something to try to find us. This evolution took about two hours for each pass and the tension aboard *Dolphin* became acute. In addition to pale complexions, our brows were beaded with moisture and shirts were dampened with sweat rings. My heart was pounding.

There was a rap on the side of the hull that became a scraping sound.

Mr. Molloy, who was the battle stations diving officer, said, "It sounds like the Japs are trying to snag us with some sort of grappling hooks and we're powerless to avoid it. Sitting on the bottom we can't maneuver and get out of the way."

They had to have spotted the debris from the small boat locker, and coupled with the oil slick we were undoubtedly leaving, had proof positive that they had a submarine, at least damaged and on the bottom. Now it looked as if they might have found us. Our tensions rose still further during the next few hours as we could tell that the Japs were trying their best to snag us.

As the scraping sound grew louder, Ding-Dong reported from the conning tower that he felt what seemed to be a jerk or a tugging. We called for the Captain who didn't respond but the Exec raced up the ladder to the conning tower and listened. Mr. Bass ordered us to clear everything we could out of the conning tower, charts, binoculars, navigation tables and logs. A feverish activity followed as we stripped the conning tower of everything we could. The guys in the control room were catching the logs and data tables we threw down from the conning tower. Binoculars, sextants and virtually everything that was not nailed down. We had already disconnected the steering stand in the forward part of the bridge, standard procedure upon diving, and now we disconnected the steering to the conning tower relying solely on the control room steering gear. On the newer boats there was no steering on the forward part of the bridge. The Bureau of Ships believed that the helmsman had no need to see where he was going. All he had to do was follow his orders. I fully agreed with that. It was one more piece of gear that didn't need to be adjusted, maintained or repaired. In fact, as a helmsman which I was, it was difficult to follow orders when they appeared to me to be wrong.

We insured that the conning tower hatch to the bridge was dogged securely and abandoned it. We shut and dogged the hatch to the control room. The Exec said to pass the word that all hands should stand by for an explosion and be prepared to take damage control action. He told Chief Brown to spread the word throughout the ship to all hands by word of mouth and not by the 1MC.

I knew we were in deep trouble. The Japanese knew they had a submarine on the bottom when their depth charging hadn't resulted in much more debris reaching the surface. Since the place we bottomed was relatively narrow, the Japs could drag a line and find us fairly easily, which was exactly what they were doing.

We had been down more than fourteen hours and the air was foul. Mr. Bass ordered the smoking lamp extinguished and gave the order for all hands not manning a battle station to lie down in their bunks. Several of the guys were showing signs of agitation. Mr. Bass told the Captain that he was having the crew spread out soda lime on the bunks and mess tables to absorb carbon dioxide and bleed in aviator's breathing oxygen to alleviate the problem. We normally carried the oxygen bottles strapped to the overhead in various compartments. The Captain nodded his concurrence.

I whispered to Mr. Holman, "What do you think our chances are?"

"Your guess is as good as mine. If the Japs wanted to force us to surface they might keep dropping depth charges but maybe just lie-to and wait until they hear us move or until we run out of air and are forced to surface."

"It doesn't look good, does it?"

"I don't hold out much hope for us at this point but maybe we could battle surface and at least give them a run for their money for a while."

"I hope we don't have to."

"Neither do I. We'd be running away and our deck gun faces forward and can't be trained to fire aft at some one who is chasing us."

Shortly we heard a kind of whirring sound that got louder and louder and. there was a loud clank as some thing hit the bridge.

The Exec shouted, "*Pass the word. Brace yourselves.*"

Before the word could be passed over the sound powered phones...

Blam!

An extremely loud explosion rocked the boat violently. It left our ears ringing. Smitty, who was at his station on the bow planes, screamed. He had blood running out both his ears. All of us had our ears ringing and were badly shaken up. Every one I saw looked pale. I was probably white as a sheet too. I even felt pale if that's possible. My stomach was queasy and I thought I'd vomit. My ears were still ringing but thank God they weren't bleeding like Smitty's.

The Exec ordered damage reports from all compartments. Light bulbs smashed, several of valve wheel handles had popped off their stems, and the cork insulation was in a shambles almost everywhere. Many cups and plates in crews mess were broken. The glass faces of both shallow water depth gauges were shattered. Incidentally, many of the souvenir glass fishing net float souvenirs fell out of lockers or off of shelves and were broken as well. The depth gauges were all out of calibration and we were using the sea pressure gauge to determine our depth.

We had one piece of good news. There was no major flooding. No significant leaks had opened up. A good sign. In one of the rare moments of silence we heard water splashing into the pump room bilges. Clyde dropped down and checked the conning tower drain. Salt water was pouring out of it. He shut the drain valve and reported that the conning tower was flooded. A bad sign. The Exec must have had a premonition that this was going to happen. He had the foresight to get the stuff we might need out of there. I wondered how we were going to get out of this mess?

With the conning tower flooded we couldn't use the periscopes. We were blind. Some other submarines had a periscope in the control room as well as one in the conning tower but not in the newer boats. Even if we had one in the control room we couldn't have use it under these conditions. It, in all likelihood, would have been smashed in the explosion as well. The Exec said we would stand fast for another hour or so and stop what leaks we could. Mr. Bass asked the COB, Chief Brown, to get the cooks to make some sandwiches and have the mess-cooks pass them out to the crew. The chief got word to the cooks and in short order we had ham and cheese sandwiches. Those of us who could hold something down attempted to eat. Several guys were already puking into buckets.

At that point of time, Mr. Bass looked around and asked, "Where'd the Captain go?"

He was missing and none of us were aware he had left the compartment. He had been leaning his elbows on the master gyro table with his chin resting in his hands. He looked to me as if he had been thinking. Now he wasn't there. We were so caught up in our reaction to our latest disaster that we hadn't noticed the Captain leaving the compartment. Mr. Bass went forward to the wardroom and when he came back he looked worried. He told Lieutenant Molloy to take charge while he looked for the Captain and headed aft. Curious, I followed him. We found the Captain in the crews mess shutting one of the emergency blow valves. That valve was supposed to stay open when ever we were rigged-for-dive. Mr. Bass got busy opening the port blow valve. He noticed me and asked me to open the starboard valve apparently already shut by the Captain. I opened it and Mr. Bass asked me to give him a hand.

When we finished opening the valves, we turned around and found that the Captain had disappeared again. The Exec asked me to follow him and headed aft toward the engine rooms where we found the Captain shutting a valve. He instructed the men in the engine room to double check their "Rig-for-Dive Bill and carefully but gently escorted Captain Malvern forward to his state room in the forward battery compartment. The Captain could be heard muttering as they headed forward. I knew the Captain had lost his marbles.

Mr. Bass called everyone who had been in the previous meeting to the control room since most of us were already there. He told us that the Captain was not well and that he was assuming command for the time being. He told Chief Brown to spread the word about the Captain to the rest of the crew. The Exec said the Japanese were reasonably assured that they had a disabled a submarine and would now get salvage ships and some hard hat divers over us soon; probably the next morning. It was imperative that we move out of here and now.

"It's going to be difficult for us to move with the conning tower flooded even with blowing all ballast tanks."

"Mr. Holman, you must have forgotten we have a safety tank that when blown dry compensates for a flooded conning tower."

"I was also thinking about the fact that we cannot use either of our periscopes."

"We'll face that problem after we surface."

You could tell by Mr. Holman's remark how badly shaken up we were. We weren't thinking.

Mr. Bass agreed with Lt. Molloy's opinion that since we were of riveted construction, there was little doubt that our fuel ballast tanks were leaking diesel fuel and we had to get out into faster moving water to carry away the oil and allow the waves to break up the slick. He said it was our only hope for survival but it was a good one.

Lt. Molloy said he thought he could handle the trim and compensation OK, but he wondered if the destruction on the bridge would cause our radio antennas and life lines to foul our propellers or our stern planes. He mentioned that the strong current would have probably caused those lines to stream aft since we had been heading into the current. The Exec said that was a good point and we would watch out for that. He said we'd wait until well after sunset before surfacing.

Mr. Bass posed the question of the best way we could conn the ship after surfacing. Lt. Molloy thought the ship could be conned on the surface from the forward torpedo room hatch using the sound powered phones. He added that it would help if we had a compass and we would use relative bearings when referring to contacts or landmarks as usual. Our basic courses would be taken off of the master gyro in the control room. Clyde said he could mount the magnetic compass from the control room in the escape trunk and compensate it as well. Ltjg Holman said that the windlass room off of the escape trunk would be good place for a phone talker. The windlass room was a water tight compartment above the forward part of the forward torpedo room which housed the anchor handling gear. The *Dolphin* was the last submarine in our navy to have a windlass room.

Communications could then be established to relay orders to the control room and maneuvering room. Mr. Bass was a good communicator. He told the chief to ensure that all hands knew what we were about to do. It would make a difference in our getting away in one piece or not surviving.

Chapter VII: The Exodus

The *Dolphin* desperately needed to surface. We needed to charge the batteries which were well depleted by now because of our high speed underwater spurts which drain the battery rapidly. All hands needed fresh air. It was more than 18 hours since we had been under attack.

The Exec asked, "What time is sunset?"

"Sunset is about 1845 and there is no moon tonight," I replied.

"That's fine. Too bad we no longer have the JK sonar to tell us if we have any rain squalls we could duck into."

"We can hope and pray for that kind of luck but I'm more concerned about the damage causing our screws to be come fouled," added Mr. Molloy.

"Here's what I propose we do."

Mr. Bass was verbalizing the plan that he had formulated. I assume he was looking for confirmation or exposure of any flaws in his proposal.

"We will prepare to surface starting at 1745. We will try to hover at about 100 feet and listen all around. If it appears clear we will continue to surface. Once on the surface we will take the best look around we can and if it looks free and dark enough the repair party will go out on deck with the primary objective of making sure that our screws are not fouled. With the distinct possibility of our radio antennas, cables and life lines lying over the side of the ship, I share Mr. Molloy's concern about the possible of fouling our propellers. We will surface without using the screws. All communications will be by the sound powered phones. Any comments from anyone?"

No one spoke up.

"We are in a precarious situation and I want all hands to know what we are about to do. We need every one to be at peak alert now. Chief Brown, see that the crew gets the word."

"Yes, sir!"

The Exec was a master at communications. I learned a lot from him about communicating with a crew. He was aware of the need-to-know about more of the details of what's going on, of every man aboard.

"Inform Maneuvering that we are going to surface without propulsion but stand by to answer bells on the battery. Remind all hands that we are still at battle stations."

The word was passed throughout the ship that we were about to head out of here and surface. It seemed to shake the lethargy most of us had fallen into. The ship seemed to come alive again. Lt. Molloy started pumping water out of Negative tank and the trim tanks. After a brief pause to see if there was any reaction from the Japanese on the surface, he ordered the safety tank blown with high pressure air. When the safety tank gauge indicated empty, we started to rise slowly. The bow rose first and we began to get a large up-angle. Water in the bilges (from the leaks in the after Torpedo and Engine rooms) had caused us to be heavy aft and that accounted for the up-angle.

Lt. Molloy used the noisy trim pump to move water from after trim tank to sea again and that leveled us off. He pumped water from auxiliary tanks to sea again to help our upward movement. He was worried about the Japanese hearing us but it was imperative that we get rid of the water in the bilges before it reached the generators or motors and shorted them out or grounded them. The drain pump couldn't get a suction in the engine rooms or the torpedo rooms because the strainers were clogged with debris from the cork insulation shredded by the blast.

The engineering officer ordered, "Chief Walton. Have all the available crew form a bucket brigade. Use buckets, pots and pitchers or what ever you can get to move as much water as you can as fast as you can from aft to the pump room bilges. Now!"

"Aye, Aye, sir!"

The chief and the messenger of the watch started taking action. The pump room bilges were smaller and the first to be cleaned.. It took a lot of time for the crew to get the water from the engine room bilges in order to get to the strainers on the suction lines but they got the job done. Clyde had rigged up a strainer that they poured the water in to remove any debris that had been carried forward.

As we rose the *Dolphin* started to swing to port. The Captain, who had appeared unnoticed, suddenly and ordered, *"Port ahead one third. Right full rudder!"*

"All stop!" Mr. Bass quickly countermanded.

"It doesn't look like our port screw was fouled," added Lt. Molloy sarcastically.

I was thinking the same thing and part of my tension was relieved.

"Do you have the conn, Captain?" asked the Exec.

"No... ah, er, no. Carry on."

"Aye, aye, sir."

Mr. Bass then called the Corpsman to the control room. He arrived fast. It was as if he had anticipated the problem. He and the Exec escorted Captain Malvern to his state room where, I believe, the Corpsman gave the Captain a shot to put him to sleep.

The *Dolphin* wallowed from side to side as we rose to the surface. We were tense not knowing what we were about to face. The ship swung to port again. *Dolphin* was now 180 degrees away from the heading we were on when we were on the bottom. The Exec told Lt. Molloy to report on possible fouling of the propellers first thing. He told Maneuvering to stand by to answer bells on the battery.

No depth gauge was needed to tell us we were on the surface. We had surfaced crossways to the strong current and rocked heavily from side to side in the swell. The damage control party was assembled in the forward torpedo room. They were all wearing life jackets. They cracked open the forward torpedo room hatch. The air pressure that had built up during our long time down whistled out. It seemed forever till the pressure equalized. While waiting we had visions of a Japanese destroyer or two waiting nearby with their guns pointed at us. Tension was extremely high.

The repair party went out on deck leaving the hatch behind them shut but not dogged. A torpedo man stood by to dog the hatch in case we had to dive or if we took a pooper wave over the bow. As much as we hated to think about it the repair party was indeed considered expendable.

It was black, raining, and windy, thank God. I recalled the first line of an old story, *It was a dark and stormy night...* Visibility was poor. A gale had whipped up while we were on the bottom and that was what apparently threw the Japs off. The froth of the surface water did a lot to disburse the diesel oil we were leaking. Thank the good Lord we weren't leaking that heavy Bunker-C oil the surface ships use. In the control room we were awaiting to hear the extent of the damage. Lt. Molloy sent word back with Clyde. Clyde was sopping wet. There appeared to be no destroyers in the immediate vicinity; good news. The damage to the bridge superstructure was extensive and much of the cables and antennas were directly above the engine rooms; bad news. Clyde said the radio antennas were not near the screws so far but if we got any headway on they would be. They had to cut them loose. Clyde grabbed two large bolt cutters out of the Pump Room and raced back topside.

The Exec, who was now back in the control room, said, "We need to get a battery charge started and now."

At this point we had to pack some amps in the battery in case we had to dive again. The electricians had reported that they had to jump several cells and if possible they would like to get in an equalizer charge.

"Sir, I think it would be a good idea if we sent word up to Lt. Molloy that we are about to start a battery charge."

"Thank you, Mr. Holman. I had overlooked that little detail."

"I just thought that it wasn't a good idea to startle Lt. Molloy and the repair party. They are working directly above the engine exhausts. We're all pretty up tight right now."

I thought it was a very smart idea considering how tense we all were but we desperately needed to get some "juice" into the batteries if indeed we could. The Exec sent a messenger up to tell the repair party what we were going to do.

Now that we were surfaced and the damage repair crew seemed to have the most critical problems under control some one had to be conning the ship from the forward torpedo room hatch. That task fell to Mr. Holman and myself. Huddled in the lee of the hatch and wearing rain slickers we attempted to see where we were going. All we could tell was that there was no land ahead of us within 5,000 yards or so. Our binoculars were almost useless. The telephone talker, huddled in the windlass room, seemed to be fairly comfortable and was out of the rain. Riding cross ways to the chop made us roll most uncomfortably. A person could become seasick. I heard that a couple of the guys were already kneeling at the thrones in the head. Word was sent down by the repair party about an hour later that all wires and cable in a position to foul the screws had been jettisoned. We could now maneuver the ship. The Exec ordered all ahead one third on the battery and right full rudder to head us into the swell and away from possible trouble. Our position in the hatch immediately improved.

Mr. Bass told Maneuvering to stand by to answer bells on two main engines and start a battery charge on two engines. He gave the order to open the main induction. When they tried to open the high induction, required before starting the engines, it grumbled, made a grinding noise, and stopped. When they opened the air intakes in the engine room, they spewed salt water. The explosion or depth charging had done something to prevent the air induction from opening completely. Apparently the induction piping had also been severely damaged. The diesels needed air as do all internal combustion engines. Now we had no choice but to draw air through the boat from the forward torpedo room hatch. All compartments were told of the problem and of the action we were about to take. All hands started securing light weight articles that were adrift so they wouldn't become a problem by clogging the engine air intake screens. When the first engine started ,paper, cork ,and other debris would be sucked up in the torrent of air flowing through the ship.

"Maneuvering. Control. Answer bells on one main engine. Commence a battery charge on three main engines," ordered the Exec.

"Helmsman, make your course 090."

"Course 090, Aye, aye, sir."

"I'm going to stay on one engine until the repair party comes below. Then I'll increase to two engine speed."

As the first engine started up we could hear and feel the vibrations through the ship. It made me feel a little more comfortable. Shortly after starting the charge, maneuvering reported one of the charging engines was out of commission. Those damn diesels were giving us trouble again and at the worst possible time.

The new course headed us directly into the waves and things settled down. We couldn't see land from the torpedo room hatch and it was dark out. We had no idea where the current had taken us. We headed east and into the current. Mr. Bass then ordered soundings taken. Even though the soundings would make a little noise, I thought it was a good idea because we weren't sure where we were. I was surprised that the fathometer was still working after all that depth charging. The soundings showed that we had 400 to 500 feet of water under our keel. The Exec's main worry at this time, he said, was that we might take water through the forward Torpedo Room hatch.

The repair party came back down about an hour later. They were drenched and bedraggled. Exhausted and bruised but otherwise OK. Mr. Molloy reported it was dangerous working on the wrecked bridge. He said the structure appeared to be unstable. Until they could examine the superstructure under more favorable conditions, Mr. Molloy said the full extent of the damage could not be determined. In the mean time we had two engines on charge and one on propulsion making four knots heading northeast into the current. Meanwhile the Motor Machinists mates were frantically changing fuel injectors on the out-of-commission engine. The starboard propeller shaft started to squeal. Clyde reported to the Exec that the deep submergence had distorted the packing in both shafts but the starboard shaft packing was skewed to the extent there was metal rubbing against metal. It made a lot of noise. It made little difference to us while we were on the surface but submerged it would be able to be heard by the destroyers, probably loud and clear.

Mr. Holman and I continued our watch in the forward torpedo room hatch. We stuck our heads out of the hatch to keep a lookout for ships and fishing boats but rain limited our visibility. I became jittery because our low range of visibility meant we might be surprised by a Japanese ship close aboard at any minute. We weren't sure we could dive this bucket of bolts, that the *Dolphin* had become, if we had to. Mr. Holman had lots of good things to say about Lt. Molloy's abilities as Engineering Officer. He was impressed with his trim control. (I keep referring to Holman as Mr. because that was how we were supposed to address junior officers.)

The rain stopped about 0400, and at dawn we got a good fix on the same island where we made landfall when we first arrived in the area. Changing course we came to 085 degrees true and headed toward the Japanese Mandated Bonin Islands. We stayed on the surface long enough after sunrise to see that we were leaking a lot of oil from our fuel ballast tanks. We were trailing a long oil slick. The Exec said that the Captain was right when he said we should stay in the fast current in order to remain undetected. Once we rounded that island we were going to be in some trouble because the current was far weaker than in the straits. It wouldn't carry the oil slick away from us as well. We tried the SD radar but it was not working. I was glad it wasn't working because I knew Brad French was right when he said he believed the Japanese could home in on it.

One of the benefits that resulted from being on the surface was the Auxiliary gang as well as the Machinists Mates were able to replace the washers, or stuffing glands, in many of the small valves that were leaking a lot easier. They were also able to clean out the debris in the bilges including the screens on the drain line suctions. Despite all the feverish work there still remained many fittings that were still leaking and much damage needed to be repaired. In the middle of all this activity word came to the control room that the copper oil line to the port main motor forward bearing had corroded through and was leaking. The bearing was getting hot. The Exec ordered the main engine declutched from the motor even though it meant we would only get propulsion from our starboard shaft. If that bearing were to wipe out we would lose our port shaft until we could get to a navy yard. Sully and another Machinist Mate got right on the job.

They had to unbolt the retainers that held the bearings in place and raise the armature of the motor a few thousandths of an inch in order to remove the lower bearing. Lowering the armature enabled them to remove the top bearing. Sully found that the babbitt metal of the bearing had just started to slough up and had it gone much farther the bearing would have been destroyed. They had to put a Prussian blue dye on the shaft and reinsert the bearings. They rotated the shaft to determine the high spots and then removed the bearings. The next step was to scape and file the blue marks off the bearings to remove the high spots. It took several times to get all the bad spots smooth. Sully spent a full twenty four hours on that job but we regained the use of the port shaft. Clyde went back and replaced the copper lube line to the bearing. While all this was going on we were fortunate we could still use the starboard shaft.

Still near the island at dawn with the weather clearing we needed to submerge. We knew that submerging this time would be hair raising. All hands had their fingers crossed on this dive. A couple of the men were fingering their rosary beads. I, for one, was extremely nervous. We had to be significantly out of trim and had no idea of how much gear was blown off the ship or the weight of the gear that had been jettisoned. We needed to know the weight in order to compute the trim. We submerged and Lt. Molloy, again made what I considered a miraculous feat of compensation. He had to do a lot of calculated guessing. It took him almost an hour to get us close to neutral buoyancy. Once the diving officer believed we were at neutral buoyancy we settled out at about ninety feet. Our steering also became much more difficult because of the drag caused by the wreckage of the bridge and the conning tower, and there was noisy rattling coming from that pile of junk that we had become. The crew was kept busy repairing a myriad of small problems, such as leaking valves the depth charging and blast had created. Fortunately, most of the internal leaks had now been completely stopped .by the diligent efforts of the Motor Machinists.

The *Dolphin* settled down uneasily at approximately 90 feet more or less. We needed to calibrate the depth gauges and that would take some time. After about twenty minutes of continuing to adjust our buoyancy the fact that we had no major flooding made us all feel somewhat better. Then...

"Conn - Sonar. Sorry I mean Control - Sonar. I have propellor noises at one eight zero."

"Very well, Sonar. Can you determine what type of contact it is?"

"Control - Sonar. I cannot tell yet. All I know is they seem to be closing slowly."

"Very well, Sonar. Keep us informed."

"Sonar–Aye."

That exchange told us that the QC sonar head still seemed to be working OK. It also told me many of the crew were not completely aware of the damage we sustained. But maybe it was just force of habit or maybe sonar didn't remember the conning tower was flooded. Technically sonar was correct since the conn of the ship was now in the control room. I found since that time that the crew was not always aware of the state of conditions in spite of the close quarters.

A few minutes later Sonar called Control stating the propellor noises appeared to be from a merchantman. The Exec ordered dead slow and we stopped every piece of gear we could and went to silent running. It would provide Sonar a better chance of determining what the approaching target was. The screws were astern of us but definitely closing. The Exec ordered us down to 175 feet. I wondered if any of the damage would choose this time to break loose and cause more leaks. Sure enough, two small valves in the engine room carried away. The motor machinists quickly pounded small plugs from their damage control kit into the hole and stopped the leak.

When the slow thump, thump, thump of the propellers got closer it became obvious it was a freighter of some kind. With no pinging and a single screw we knew it was not a destroyer. All of us in the control room breathed a sigh of relief. That relief was short lived however.

At the very moment the freighter was passing directly overhead there was the sound of a muffled explosion and we heard the word shouted, "Fire in the after battery.".

I damn near panicked. I was scared. I knew the *Dolphin* was old and tired but now it seemed that she was also jinxed. What else could go wrong?

The Auxiliary Electrician dashed back into the after battery together with the messenger of the watch. Lt. Molloy ran back after them, leaving the diving officer duties to Mr. Holman. Smoke started to come through the ventilation ducts and soon filled the control room. We looked at each other with anxiety written all over our faces. Beads of perspiration were seen on brows as well as sweat rings under arm pits. Fifteen minutes later Mr. Molloy was back with the electrician and messenger. They reported the fire was out. The electrician said a small pocket of hydrogen gas that had accumulated in the battery well during the last battery charge exploded. Some loose paint caught fire. He added that the battery ventilation system blowers had been secured during the depth charging and should have been checked open when the charge was started.

This was but another example of how unnerved we had become. The battery blowers should have been turned on and then should have turned them up to high speed during the finishing rate. The highest volume of hydrogen gas is produced when the battery charge reaches the finishing rate. During daily routine small bits of paper, cork, and hair would accumulate and cling to any loose and flaking paint. If it was near any source of ignition it would likely catch fire. It could have been devastating. Shutting off the circulating air fans and the timely use of a CO_2 extinguisher prevented a catastrophe. Smoke continued to fill the control room as the circulating air fans were turned back on.

When we submerged, the weather on the surface was clearing.

Fortunately, it was still rough and was breaking up our oil slick. By our dead reckoning plot, we were still within sight of the island and exposed to air coverage. Our fate could have been sealed if we had been forced to surface at this time. We had to bear up under the choking smoke. We badly needed to surface. We had to take a suction through the boat to clear the smoke out. It would also rid the boat of any other pockets of hydrogen gas, still lingering, that may have developed during the charge.

The Exec ordered soundings as he evaluated our situation. He said that the Captain was again right on going deep when we were trailing a large oil slick. Mr. Bass said that we would stay deep, but not as deep as usual, while we were this close to the Island. We stayed at 90 feet for the time being. The soundings indicated that we had about 300 feet under our keel and that gave us a reasonable margin of safety. Mr. Molloy requested that we surface as soon as possible. He said his men were hampered in their repair efforts by the smokey atmosphere. The Exec said he intended to surface as soon as possible but despite the choking smoke we'd have to stay submerged for a while longer; at least until sunset. Mr. Bass then ordered that the CO_2 absorbent powder be spread out again on the bunks in the after battery, the torpedo rooms and on the mess tables. Several of the men took the packages of the powder and proceeded to alleviate the situation. I don't recall that I felt any relief from the CO_2 absorbent, but I guess that it must have done some good. I did seem to feel better after they released some more aviators breathing oxygen into the boat. We had to endure the smoke and choking fumes for a while longer.

Chapter VIII: Do Not Look Back

Things quieted down after the freighter's propeller noises faded off. The smoke was still thick and some of the men on watch were lying on the padding over the steel deck plates to rest. The smoke was not as thick at that level. I looked at a couple of them and noticed they had a kind of pale, bluish complexion. Their lips had a purple tinge to them. I couldn't see them breathe. Were they passed out? Had they died? I didn't like that thought a bit. During the ensuing war, one or two submarines were lost and records did not show any attacks that could be related to their loss. Perhaps they were all overcome with carbon dioxide and went to sleep while the submarine got heavier and heavier and finally sank.

Chief Brown asked the Exec if the smoking lamp could be lit. The Exec told him to pass the word that the smoking lamp was lit for only one cigarette. Porky, who was on the bow planes, pulled one of the coffin nails out of his pack and put it in his mouth. He struck a match. The match just sputtered. There was not enough oxygen in the air to support the combustion. Mr. Bass noticed it and he immediately countermanded his order. It was really stupid to try to smoke in that already foul, smokey atmosphere. Chief Brown didn't seem to be one of those people addicted to cigarettes.

It had been fifteen and a half hours plus since we submerged. With many of the men in a semi-comatose state, Mr. Molloy asked the Exec if we could possibly surface. He said we needed to surface soon. The Exec said we should be well out of sight of land by now and it would soon be dark. He passed the word to make all preparations to surface. I thought, from what I had just witnessed, that the men slumped over the plane control wheels might not be able to obey any orders. I was not feeling very alert myself.

After listening carefully at periscope depth for about ten minutes the Exec ordered us to surface and three blasts were sounded on the klaxon. We rose with a nice, slight angle. When we broke surface, the Exec, Lt Molloy and I were in the windlass room waiting to get out on deck. The Exec told the telephone talker to tell control to start the low pressure blowers immediately. The air pressure from all the air leaks that had built up during the dive was so high we could start the blowers. It would help reduce the air pressure before we cracked the hatch. We would not have to wait as long for the pressure to equalize. As soon as we heard the low pressure blowers start we cracked the hatch and the air leaked out with the high pitched scream again. When the scream died down and the pressure equalized with the out side atmosphere we opened the hatch. Once out on deck, leaving the phone talker behind us huddled in the hatch, we saw there were a few high cumulus clouds with orange tinges on them reflecting the setting sun, but more important no airplanes, ships or land could be seen. My anxiety was eased considerably.

The first time on deck since the depth charging and explosion gave me the same sinking feeling one gets when an elevator suddenly drops too fast. I was very apprehensive. Looking at the shattered bridge I began to have serious doubts about our ability to make it all the way to Midway. We struggled up the wreckage and stood on the pile of scrap metal that used to be the bridge. It vibrated and felt shaky. I now believed that we couldn't possibly make it to Pearl Harbor. Maybe not even Midway. It seemed to me as if the *Dolphin* was a jinxed ship. We were on borrowed time. A piece of metal was dangling from a line or wire of some sort. It was swaying with the motion of the ship. It made a noise that went thunk - thunk every few minutes. It sounded like some one was trying to get out from under the wreckage. The bridge had the appearance and sounds of being haunted. It took a few minutes before we found out it was one chunk of metal banging against another. It was spooky.

The bridge was a mess. The fairwater had been shredded and the radio masts were bent at severe angles. One looking as if it were almost ready to fall off and the other bent in the opposite direction. The stand on which we mounted the signal light had only one bolt holding it to the deck. I thought about trying to salvage it for use when I spotted the light rolling between a 50cal machine gun stanchion and a brace for a foot platform. The light was smashed. I retrieved it and threw it overboard. That eliminated one source of noise. When we were submerged now we had so many rattles we sounded like a junk wagon being driven over a cobblestone street. I made a mental note to tell Clyde the platform could be thrown over the side too. Standing on what remained of the bridge we heard the engines start up. A thick cloud of white smoke from the diesel exhausts blew forward by the light breeze and engulfed the bridge wreckage. Lt. Molloy ran back to the forward torpedo room hatch and told the telephone talker to tell the electricians in the maneuvering room to adjust the engine speed and load to reduce the smoke.

Below decks a clean sweep down, fore and aft, was ordered. Several burlap bags full of cork insulation were sent topside for dumping. This time they were weighted down with broken parts and pieces of glass from the shattered gauges throughout the boat. The engines began to pull a suction through the boat as we commenced a battery charge on the two generator engines with propulsion on one of the direct drive engines. The suction started to clear the smoke out of the compartments. The small fans located in each compartment cleared out the isolated pockets that were farther away from the passage ways. Most of the men who looked so deathly pale earlier now had color returned to their faces.

The air compressors were started up to bring the 3,000 psi, high pressure air banks up to the required level. The pressure was down low from using so much air the last three times we surfaced. We had even tapped into the "Captains bank" the last time we needed to blow all main ballast tanks when we surfaced. The Captains bank was reserved for emergencies only. We had been in one hell of an emergency and as far as I was concerned we were still in one. Number one air bank was supposed to be used only on the Captain's orders. It was the only high pressure bank inside the pressure hull. The other four banks were in the ballast tanks outside the pressure hull. Each bank was composed of seven large flasks all tied in to one system and could be used separately..

After the air charge started, Clyde reported that our number one air compressor was out of commission. Either one of the depth charge attacks or the final blast had fractured the cast iron base of the compressor. Clyde said that it couldn't be repaired. Thank God we had two large air compressors. I hoped that number two air compressor wouldn't break down. Clyde started cramming air into the banks with number two. What was going to break down next?

Maneuvering sent word up to Lt. Molloy that the number four main engine was back in commission. He reported it to the Exec, recommending it be put on propulsion to give us more speed. The Exec, who had already heard the message, concurred and soon we were making a few more knots. We had to get farther away from the Japanese main islands as quickly as possible. We were about half way between Kyushu and Sofu Gan, (called Lots Wife), and right in the middle of one of the main shipping lanes from Japan. I fully expected to sight merchant ships at night and to hear them during the day if we were submerged during daylight hours.

Later that night when we reached the finishing rate on the battery charge we were able to put another engine on propulsion. That was fortunate because Mr. Holman, the officer standing watch in the forward torpedo room hatch, had spotted the lights of a ship off of our starboard quarter when he made one of our zigs to make sure the area astern of us was clear. He calculated the Closest Point of Approach (CPA) of this contact was only 2,000 yards. We could increase that distance by at least 8,000 yards from the speed now provided by the added engine on propulsion and by taking a normal escape course at ninety degrees to the projected course of the contact. The need to dive would be considerably reduced depending on whether the approaching ship was a merchantman or a warship. A merchant ship would not be likely spot a submarine or even be on watch for one, especially in "peace time"and at night. In our case, the Japanese Navy might have established a system to alert their merchant fleet to be on the alert for any submarine or other potential threats they knew about. We didn't know and we could not take a chance.

Our primary concern continued to be the Japanese navy. They may have put down some hard hat divers by this time and discovered the submarine they attacked was not there. We had to assume we were being hunted. The Exec expressed the hope the Japanese would try to drag grappling hooks again and hope to find their quarry. That would be time consuming for them and we hoped they would do just that. We continued to grind our way toward the Bonin Islands. We were making surprisingly good speed on the surface even with the starboard shaft squealing. The packing that had squeezed out around the starboard shaft became hot and started to smoke. Sully rigged up a line that sprayed a fine stream of water directly on the shaft where it went into the packing. It worked. The spray cooled it down and eliminated the smoke. It helped reduced the squealing somewhat. I'm sure we all had our fingers crossed, hoping we wouldn't lose the use of the starboard shaft. If the shaft froze up we would be in dire straights. We would lose a significant amount speed and our maneuverability would be greatly restricted. I kept my fingers tightly crossed.

The next morning we submerged again to adjust the trim of the ship in case we were spotted. If we were forced to dive and take evasive action we needed to uncover any hidden problems and correct them before this possibility occurred. This dive, again, was a weird one. We submerged OK and at first the trim seemed fine but we kept rising after reaching periscope depth was reached. We had to speed up, plane down, and flood our trim tanks constantly. Lt. Molloy finally figured out it was the conning tower that gave us the problem. The water that flooded in after the blast had leaked out while we were on the surface. It took time to fill up again giving us an erroneous impression we had miscalculated our trim. When the conning tower got fully flooded again we had to pump water out of our trim tanks to get close to neutral buoyancy .

There was a door in the after end of the conning tower. It was used only when we were at battle stations - surface. The men could get to the deck gun faster. It had been sprung by the explosion and was absolutely useless. Mr. Molloy suggested the door be pried open and secured to speed the flooding in the event we had to submerge. The Exec endorsed the idea and the Motor Machinists took the necessary action after we surfaced. We plodded steadily along toward the widest gap in the Bonins. We spotted a contact astern of us that was hull down on the horizon. It gave us a scare when it seemed to change course in our direction. It was too bad that we couldn't use either of the periscopes to look for contacts. It would have given us a greater height of eye and enabled us to detect contacts much farther away. As this contact came closer we could clearly see the masts and king posts of a freighter. Our concern abated some when it turned away. It may have been trying to avoid a fishing fleet that may have been in its way.

I'm told that a merchantman occasionally might actually try to avoid small craft if they ever became alert enough to use eye sight instead of relying on their automatic pilots. I had heard that the Japanese were pretty faithful to the rules of the road in that regard. The record for their merchant marine was pretty good on that score.

At the end of his watch, Ltjg Holman came back to the control room. He complained about standing watch in the forward torpedo room hatch. He said he couldn't see behind us and every time we zigged to see what was in our blind sector, it slowed us down considerably. He suggested it would help if we could station another lookout in the after torpedo room hatch. The Exec rejected that as much too dangerous. A sweeping wave could pour tons of water into our boat and reduce our positive buoyancy to zero or wash the lookouts over the side if we had the hatch shut. I mentally agreed. However, this close to Japan, I worried that we wouldn't be able to see a destroyer creeping up on us. Our sonar's poorest listening area lay directly astern. Mr. Bass had also mentioned his concern about our blind spot. Sonar was at its poorest when underway on the surface. It was virtually useless. Suspecting that the Japanese could home in on our SD Radar we didn't dare try to use it this close to land. In fact we weren't sure the radar was even working.

Lt. Molloy, agreed with Mr. Holman saying every time we made zigs to clear our stern we lost time and wasted fuel. Yet, he said, it was essential for us to cover our blind spot. It was critical we remain undetected until we got within radio range of Midway. He suggested we might be able to man the bridge again if we could get the 7MC working or even get a sound powered phone up there. He said we could cover our blind sector from that slightly elevated vantage point with no obstructions astern of us. He added that the decking needed to be repaired somewhat so we would be able to use it without so much danger to anyone standing watch on the bridge. The bridge decking had been shredded from the blast and there was no safe place to stand and that was a problem. Clyde and Mr. Molloy went up to the bridge with the Exec's approval and looked the situation over. When they came back down Clyde said that he could fabricate a sheet metal platform that would serve satisfactorily by welding a couple of braces and a pair of cross beams to the existing stanchions. Clyde was damn good at makeshift repairs.

Brad suggested it wouldn't be too hard to install a jack for a sound powered phone on the wrecked bridge if we couldn't get the 7MC working again. Lt. Molloy said he thought the idea would work. The Exec put his stamp of approval on it. He agreed that a bridge watch was essential to our survival but added that at no time would it consist of more than two people. An Officer of the deck and a lookout. Clyde did an excellent job of fabricating a three foot by six foot piece of sheet metal and attaching it to the wreckage.

Brad found the 7MC on the bridge couldn't be easily repaired but he said he would continue to work on it. However he thought it would definitely be possible to install a sound powered phone jack up there if they could find a suitable conduit to run the line. Clyde and Sully put their heads together and after checking the blueprints and tinkering around they found a cable trunk that could be adapted to serve the purpose. With a little cutting, tugging and pulling they got a jack box for a sound powered phone bolted to the side of the steering stand on the forward part of the bridge. Brad wired it up quickly. It tested out fine. That was typical of the things the *Dolphin's* crew could do when the chips were down.

    Chief Walton, our Chief electrician, said he thought it was too dangerous to put men up on the bridge and expect them to pass the word to dive and still run fast enough to make it to the forward torpedo room hatch in time. Mr. Bass's normally ruddy complexion deepened perceptibly as he told the chief, in strong language but ever so politely, that every officer and man aboard would consider himself expendable if it meant saving the *Dolphin*. Chief Walton, who's face was now red, agreed that Mr. Bass was right.

    Mr. Holman and I were the first to stand watch on the wreck of the bridge. We felt we were pioneers being the first to stand watch in two unique situations. First in the forward torpedo room hatch and now on the wrecked bridge. It was very nerve wracking and took some getting used to. We had a following sea and a light breeze which fortunately kept the bridge dry. We weren't plowing into the waves which helped ease things. My mind worked over-time. I was afraid the vibrations I felt through the soles of my feet were those of the shattered bridge and conning tower which were about to slide over the side and into the ocean taking me and Mr. Holman with them. Added to this feeling were all sorts of moans and groans coming from the wreckage, the source of which were unknown. This made the watch harrowing for me and my imagination.

    The jury-rigged communication system had some problems that had to be worked out. We needed the line clear for communications to and from the bridge to the control room and the maneuvering room. All other communications below were done by the 7MC, which was now in operation below decks and by the sound powered phones had not failed. The sound powered phones which had not failed were always reliable. We had to alert the below decks watch by phone of any contacts that could possibly force us to dive. The electricians in the maneuvering spaces were on the line and heard any orders from the bridge directly. The control room watch also heard the orders. It worked very well. Brad said he thought he could find a way to get the 7MC on the bridge working.

The officers held a conference in the wardroom to discuss if there was a need to dive at all. Mr. Bass said that we were short on time. Diving would slow us up considerably and we would lose less diesel oil, while on the surface, which was becoming a limiting factor. The Exec said with a good pair of lookouts and an occasional use of the radar, if it could be repaired, we should give it a try. Since our track to Midway was well to the north of the main shipping lanes we should encounter few ships. So we added another lookout to the bridge watch. We were becoming less and less fearful of another Japanese attack.

I worked on the charts with Mr. Bass and plotted the fix he obtained from his star sights, which were good since the weather had cleared and we had a well defined horizon at sunset as well as sunrise. Good weather was something we could not always depend on. Thank God the Exec had the foresight to get the navigation tables and the sextants out of the conning tower before the blast caused the compartment to be flooded. Our plotted position on the chart fell one hundred and ten nautical miles southwest of Sofu Gan. An island called "Lot's Wife." We should pass about thirty miles or so south of the island. This was a bit close, I thought, but with luck we would probably encounter only a few fishing boats. We knew of no naval base or naval activity on or around Sofu Gan.

The next morning, Mr. Molloy, after checking out the engine air induction system below decks, said that he thought that the system looked too bad to try to take air through the induction piping. He asked the Exec for permission to answer bells on the battery. He wanted to go topside and check out the high induction and its related piping below the deck superstructure without smoke from the engines interfering. Permission was granted and a close inspection by Mr. Molloy determined that the system could not be operated. It needed substantial repairs. We would have to endure the constant flow of air through the boat. The air whistling through the boat was irritating and a bit chilly Anyone who could moved away from the flow of air to keep warm. Some even dropped down into the pump room to grab some "z's." The closer you were to the air flow the colder it was. As far as the conning tower was concerned there was no way we could occupy it. The hatch from the bridge to the conning tower was so badly sprung that we could neither open it nor close it. We needed a new conning tower. A shipyard had to build and pressure test it.

We stayed on the surface and continued toward Midway. The sea state was now almost calm and we could clearly see the oil slick trailing behind us. The Pacific Ocean was behaving itself again, thank you. About mid morning Mr. Holman, who was the Officer of the Deck, spotted a tall white object poking its head above the horizon off the port bow. I immediately identified it as Sofu Gan. As the tip of the island came abeam a little closer you could see that it was a huge volcanic rock covered with bird guano. Indeed, it looked like a pillar of salt. That's why old time sailors called the island Lot's Wife. Many of the old whalers were religious as well as superstitious. In the Old Testament of the Bible, Lot's wife turned to look back at the town of Sodom which she was forbidden to do and the Lord turned her into a pillar of salt. I thought of something else I read in the Bible. When I got off watch, I went below, picked up a Bible, and turned to Luke.

"No one who puts his hand to the plow and looks back is fit for the kingdom of God.".

I puzzled over that sentence for years. A farmer friend of mine told me later it meant you had to keep you're eyes focused ahead of you when you were plowing in order to plow a straight line. It was peculiar how the phrase "looks back" stuck in my mind. I never looked back at Sofu Gan again.

The next morning, after the island had dropped through the horizon astern of us, I relieved Ding-Dong on the wrecked bridge at the end of his watch. He climbed down off the bridge and was walking to the forward torpedo room hatch to go below when a freak wave washed over the deck. We lost sight of him and were about to commence our *man overboard* procedure. There was a doubt in my mind that we could even do that procedure considering our lack of practice and the *Dolphin's* poor materiel condition. Then I spotted a pair of hands on the lower of the two life lines on the starboard side by the four inch deck gun. As I craned to get a better look I saw that Ding-Dong was hanging on for dear life. The OOD, Mr. Holman, turned the ship to port to put him in the lee of the waves and wind and went to "All stop."

Mr. Holman's call on the sound powered phones brought quick results. I scrambled down to the deck and grabbed one of his arms. Two men came up from the forward torpedo room and together we helped Ding-Dong back up on deck. He seemed to be all right. Soon Clyde and Porky came topside and strung a life line from the side of the bridge to the forward torpedo room hatch. That line should have been put up days ago. The normal life lines lining the sides of the deck had been blown off by the blast back at Kagashima or were jettisoned. Now we were all ordered to wear life vests when we went topside. Those kapok vests were of very little use, they were so compacted that they had little buoyancy. One of the guys in the crew said that the best use we could make of then would be as weights for the garbage sacks we tossed it over the side. He said if he ever got washed over the side with one of those on, the first thing he'd do was to get rid of it.

Things were assuming a routine of sorts. The watch sections had assumed their regular duties, and although the repairs and clean up were still factors, we had a sense of being back on a routine. The officers were paired up with different chiefs in their watch sections and that alone seemed to erase or dim their recent nervousness. Most of us were worrying about what was going to happen next. Captain Malvern had not made an appearance in days. I didn't even see him when I went up to the Wardroom to wind the chronometers which I still had to do. The radiomen couldn't get me a time tic so I couldn't adjust our chronometers. I could only wind them. We had to hope they would continue to keep accurate time. Smitty was complaining that his ears were still ringing and it made him dizzy. He had to be taken off the watch list. All the other cuts and bruises on various guys seemed to be healing OK. A number of bandages covering small cuts could be seen among the officers and men but we were lucky that only one of us had broken a bone. Johnson's forearm.

We had now been leaking oil from the distorted or sprung rivets in our fuel ballast tanks for three days. The engineer, Mr. Molloy, said if the leakage rate continued he didn't believe we could make it to Midway. When I heard that I thought wouldn't it be ironic if we had to abandon ship in the middle of nowhere and have no chance of rescue after the Japanese gave us such a severe beating and still couldn't destroy us in their own home waters. The thought of our plight went through my mind and I flashed back to my sighting of the flash of blue-green light that first evening at sea. Then I thought again of St Elmo's fire shining on my face that night on the bridge off of Kagoshima. Would that cancel out the blue-green light? Which of these omens would come to pass? The good luck of the blue green light or the bad luck of the white light of St. Elmo's fire

Chapter IX: This Too Shall Pass

Mr. Bass and I were in the control room going over the charts showing the currents in the Northern Pacific to see if we could find a current nearby that we could ride to get to Midway faster. It would help us to conserve our precious fuel. There were several major currents that were quite strong heading east. Some had speeds of up to four knots. We were close to a three knot current and proceeded to alter our course slightly to take advantage of it.

While we were studying the charts, Lt. Molloy came charging into the compartment with a set of blueprints. He had been pouring over our overhaul records back in the maneuvering spaces. He excitedly told the Exec that two of our larger fuel oil ballast tanks had been welded to correct a major leak we had at one time. He said it was done during the *Dolphin's* last overhaul at Mare Island. If the tanks were still intact, we could pump the remaining diesel oil into them. We checked it out at once and found the two tanks did not appear to be leaking. They were definitely the tanks that had been welded at Mare Island. A further check confirmed they were not leaking. We pumped as much of the diesel oil into the two tanks as we could. When most, if not all, of the remaining diesel oil was transferred into them it would help extend our range considerably.

At first glance it looked good. When transfer of fuel was completed it boosted the morale of the entire crew considerably. One of the leaking tanks was a fuel ballast tank now empty. We were able to convert it to a regular ballast tank by removing a blank from a vent valve. A couple of the Motor Machinists spent an hour topside underneath the after superstructure making the conversion. The tank now could be blown dry and give the *Dolphin* more buoyancy. The next morning we trailed far less oil than before. The oil slick we had been leaving was now considerably smaller. We finally began to believe that we'd get to Midway. Now I knew we'd get there. I thought of my good luck omen on the first evening we left Pearl. The flash of blue-green light on the horizon at sunset. Apparently my good luck charm was not offset by the bad luck omen of St. Elmo's fire but I still had my fingers crossed.

Later on that day, Mr. Molloy approached the Exec with an idea.

"Sir. If we can displace less water we wouldn't lose so much fuel and we could extend our range even farther."

"How do you suggest we do that, Mr. Molloy?"

"We could jettison the three torpedoes in the deck locker. If they were hot runs they would be no good anyway. Chief Brown reminded me that they could be dumped over the side with no danger."

"Can't do that, Mr. Molloy. We have to account for every torpedo we took aboard and have good reasons for getting rid of them."

"Isn't this mess we're in a good enough reason?"

"Not to the top brass. They think only in terms of the cost of each torpedo. Sorry but we can't do that."

"Oh well, we're only talking about 3 or 4,000 pounds anyway."

That ended that. No mention was made as to whether they posed any hazard to us from an explosion. They weren't armed. They couldn't have been. There were no exploders in their warheads.

Two days later we were within 250 miles of Midway. We hadn't been sighted by the Japanese and all we saw were a few albatross. The Executive Officer was concerned that Midway might need to be prepared for us. In our trashed condition I was afraid we might look like some strange foreign weapon and Midway might assume we were hostile. Depending on the international situation, it seemed possible that we might be attacked when we got close to the island. I had different thoughts. We had no communications about the outside world for several weeks. Who knows what was going on in the world? How was the war in Europe going? For all we knew the Germans could have invaded England by now.

Mr. Bass asked the communications officer, Ltjg Ward, if he could jury-rig an antenna so we could radio Midway. Mr. Ward had also been on the Naval Academy football team. I believe he was in the backfield. He said he was already working on it but we needed to weld a stanchion to the deck to string an antenna. Mr. Bass told him to make it so. From time to time Mr. Ward gave us some training from the booklet, *Reef Points*, that was issued to him when he was at the academy. It had humorous questions the plebes were required to know the answer to when an upper class man asked them. Questions like, "How's the cow, Mr.?" or "What time is it, Mr.?"

Clyde and a couple of other Auxilliarymen took acetylene tanks, torches, and pipes topside. In a couple of hours they had a mast attached to the after deck. It took some doing. They had to cut through the wooden decking and weld one of the pipes to the hull. Inserting a long rod they welded it to the pipe. It took two or three pieces of angle iron welded to the conning tower fair water to stabilize the fabricated mast. The radio men strung up the length of antenna wire we needed and secured it aft with an insulated bracket. Everything was fine except for the insulator where the antenna lead passes into the ship. We had two insulators on the fair water; one for the regular radio transmitter and one for the radar. They both were shattered during the depth charging or the grappling hook bomb; more likely the latter.

I was a safety watch for Brad while he was trying to connect up the jury-rigged antenna. He was scratching his head trying to think of what he could use in place of the shattered insulator. A few minutes later, Porky, who was heading up to the bridge to stand watch came aft and asked the "stupid" question:

"What are you guys trying to do?"

"Porky, Brad's got a problem here. Let him figure it out."

"I was just asking."

"Get your ass up on the bridge and stand you're watch. That is, unless you want a size twelve shoe up you're butt. OK?"

Porky shrugged his shoulders and started to head up to his watch.

"Porky, we need something to replace this insulator."

Brad then patiently told him in detail what the problem was and showed him the broken pieces of the insulator.

Porky, ignoring my threat, said, "I carried one of those things aboard when we were in Mare Island."

"You what?"

"When we loaded stuff at Mare Island I carried a lot of radio stuff aboard."

"Where did you put it?" asked Brad.

"In the ammo locker in the after torpedo room just where you told me to."

With all the turmoil Brad had forgotten he had stored some gear back aft in the ship's magazine spaces. He raced away and was right back with the insulator. Within the hour the insulator was installed and we were in touch with Midway. Thank God the radiomen had done so much work on drying out the radio trunk and eliminating most of the tricky grounds.

When he finished with the radio antenna, Brad took a look at the radar antenna. He asked Clyde if he could bend the antenna mounting bracket a little more toward the vertical. It was on the after side of the now wrecked starboard radio mast. Clyde got it almost vertical using a huge pipe wrench. Brad then asked permission to try out the radar. After a brief test Brad reported that the radar was now working fine even with the shattered insulator. The next day it gave us a good picture of aircraft probably flying around Midway Island.

Our communication with the atoll was peculiar. The people at Midway behaved strangely. They seemed to treat us as an alien force, as I suspected they might, but not as an enemy. About an hour after we were in contact with the island, a PBY came over, circled us several times and then left heading, I presumed, back to Midway. Since we no longer resembled the profile of any known U.S. submarine, it took some doing to get them to recognize us and take our messages seriously. I went below and dug out the biggest American flag we had on board. With the Exec's permission I had it

TOP SECRET

flying from the highest part of our wrecked superstructure. We finally convinced them we were an authentic U.S. Navy submarine. Several different types of airplanes were now flying and looking us over. I wondered if it was mere curiosity or were they really on alert for a possible enemy attack ?

The brass on Midway apparently had no knowledge of our mission. They had to check us out with the Commander of the Submarine Scouting Force - Pacific or at least with our squadron commander. With Midway now in sight, we asked for confirmation that a message had been sent to Pearl stating that the *Dolphin* had reached Midway. That confirmation took nearly four hours. It seemed that the secrecy of our mission had been well kept. I was puzzled. I thought that the Admiral, or at the very least our Division Commander, would have taken steps to see that we were properly welcomed back. I believed that orders should have been given to render all possible aid and assistance. A reception committee should have been arranged. I believed the brass would want to get all of the information we learned from our patrol. Mr. Bass said he had no idea who would get the message that we were at Midway and the word might not get to our Squadron or Division Commanders.

At last Midway sent a message, they would send out a team to see what could be done for us. They told us we couldn't enter the lagoon because they were dredging the channel. The *Dolphin* waited and waited. Lying-to in the undulant swell of the Pacific Ocean became uncomfortable. We were trying to conserve our diesel fuel in case we had to go on our own to Pearl. It was too deep to anchor so we had to answer bells on the battery to keep us heading into the swell. During the day we were close enough to the island that we could see planes taking off and landing on the air strip. I identified a Boeing Flying Fortress bomber, a Grumman Wildcat fighter and a Brewster Buffalo fighter in addition to the PBY's that were circling over us constantly.

Night came and still no assistance or communications from Midway. The Exec told Mr. Ward to call the base again. The base acknowledged receipt of the message but did not otherwise respond. Finally an incoming message told us a boat would be coming out in the morning with repair and logistics people aboard. A motor launch was seen coming out the channel about 9 a.m., and I sarcastically wondered to myself if they had delayed long enough to have a nice leisurely breakfast. All we had was pancakes with fried Spam. We were tired and under stress, anxious to get moving again. The 50-foot motor launch came along side and about twenty sailors managed to get aboard *Dolphin* with some difficulty. Their leader was a young, thin, blond, and bespectacled Lieutenant junior grade from the communications facility. His blue eyes, framed with a pair of wire rimmed glasses, were wide with amazement at our topside condition as were the eyes of his sailors.

Submarines were always a curiosity to which the public flocked. They clucked and wagged their heads and said that they always wondered how anybody could stand to go to sea in one of those things that goes under water. These sailors from Midway were no exception. Many of them were likely convinced that they would never volunteer for submarines especially after seeing the trashed condition of the *Dolphin*.

The Lieutenant's name was Carson. I remember that he had a faint scent of after shave lotion on him. It suddenly made me aware of my own body odor. We all must have smelled like hell. I'm surprised that his nose didn't turn up. I'm sure that all hands that he came near had the same reaction as I did. None of us had a shower since our getaway from Kagashima. Lt. Carson said that one thing was for sure, he was going to tell the Base Commander about the *Dolphin's* physical condition. However he didn't hold out much hope for us in the way of assistance. He said Midway had no submarine repair facilities available and very little diesel fuel. There was no submarine tender or floating dry-dock in port and no likelihood there would be in the near future. Lt Carson told us major repair on the *Dolphin* was not possible. Food and supplies were short because the island's defenses were being bolstered. The lieutenant said he had instructions from the base commander to do what he could for us. He also informed Mr. Bass that the Commandant would like to see our Skipper. The Exec told him the Captain was ill and he would do the honors instead.

Meanwhile the sailors that Lt. Carson brought with him were working with Clyde to help clean up some of the more dangerous parts of the damaged bridge superstructure. Mr. Molloy had already prioritized the repairs we needed and that helped speed up the work. Sully had several of the sailors down below in the engine rooms to help him straighten out some of the bent and patched piping and replace the damaged valves. They said it would be necessary to put the *Dolphin* in dry-dock to correct the bearing problem in the starboard shaft as well as the damage to the sonar heads. No Floating Dry Dock was stationed at Midway. Clyde had a couple of men work on the old trim pump and the drain pump which were essential to our safe trip back to Pearl. About an hour after work started the Coxwain of the motor launch took off with about five or six sailors and headed back to the island. Clyde was supervising the repairs on deck. I asked him what was happening. He said they were going after some valves and wiring and they would be back soon.

In his visit with the Commandant, Mr. Bass told him that Captain Malvern had a nervous breakdown, and he had temporarily relieved him of command. He told him that material casualties aboard made it imperative that the Captain and two thirds of the officers and men be taken off the ship and flown to Pearl Harbor. The Exec emphasized that the *Dolphin's* condition was shaky at best and that, coupled with the low fuel supply, the *Dolphin* might not make it back to Pearl Harbor. If we had to abandon her, the Exec said, with a full crew there could be a real potential for loss of life. He recommended that if at all possible the *Dolphin* should be towed back to Pearl Harbor with only a skeleton crew aboard. Mr. Bass added that we could, if absolutely necessary, try to bring her back to Pearl by ourselves but it probably would mean losing the submarine as well as all hands aboard.

A few of our guys were on deck wearing life jackets to take in some sun and gawk at the low lying island. None of us aboard had ever set foot on the island despite the several practice patrols we had made around the area. Most of those patrols were well out of sight of

Midway and we couldn't even get a periscope view of the atoll. The work topside consisted mostly of stripping away as much of the trashed bridge structure as possible which didn't seem like a hell of a lot. Below decks the gang was busy taking damaged gear and wiring apart and getting it topside.

Lt. Carson left for the island before the noon meal. We began to believe the *Dolphin* had a future after all. It finally seemed somebody actually gave a damn. Wasting no time, the Lieutenant sent us a radio message telling us a 50-foot motor launch would come along side to take off the Captain and forty one of the crew as the Exec had requested. Mr. Bass, Lt. Molloy, and the Yeoman huddled together and quickly named those who would be off-loaded. All the men who hadn't yet attained qualified-in-submarines status and the junior least experienced men in the various ratings were the bulk of those leaving. Smitty, who's ears had bled during the explosion had been suffering from acute tinnitus (a ringing in his ears) was also on the list as was Johnson with his broken arm. Johnson was adamant that he stay aboard and was accepted. No one complained about not getting off and most of the men who had to get off complained that they wanted to stay aboard. This said something about the bonds that had been established during our ordeal. Clyde, Sully, and I were among those selected to stay aboard. The Exec, Mr. Molloy, Mr. Holman, and Ltjg Ward were the officers who stayed with us.

When Lt. Carson came back aboard he told Mr. Bass there was a tug boat intended for towing an empty aviation fuel barge back to Pearl but would take us in tow instead. The tug would be along side before 1600. The motor launch could be seen coming out the channel, and Chief Brown passed the word for everyone who was supposed to disembark to get top side. I had a brilliant idea. I dashed below and got my letter to Meilin from under my mattress, stuffed it into an envelope and hurried back up topside. The motor launch came along side as I reached the deck.

The Chief started calling out names. The Yeoman checked off their names as the Chief called them out. Mess cooks and various strikers and unqualified men were among the personnel we sent ashore. I handed my letter to Meilin to Stark, the Yeoman striker, and asked him to mail it for me as soon as he could. Maybe right here on Midway. Stark was obviously pleased to get off the ship and eagerly agreed to mail my letter. I was a little worried that he might forget to mail it but at least it was an attempt to get something to Meilin. I also suspected Stark would volunteer out of submarines. Submarines weren't his cup of tea. Captain Malvern was carefully assisted down off the deck and into the launch by the Exec. Mr. Bass saluted him as the launch pulled away. The Captain looked pale and wasn't smiling. I silently wished him well.

The tug arrived along side at 1645. It was the *U.S.S. Algorma (AT-34)*. I'll never forget that little tug. Just like "The Little Engine that Could" in the children's storybook, it was "The Little Tug that Could". They sent over two large hawsers which we threaded through our bullnose. We placed chafing gear under the hawsers so they wouldn't get worn through or abraded by wave action. We lashed the helm so the *Dolphin* wouldn't sway or veer as the tug towed us. It took some doing but by sundown we were under tow en route to Pearl Harbor wallowing behind the *Algorma* at about six knots. For all we'd been through we were happy to be going back to Pearl.

We weren't feeling a bit comfortable about the situation. Everybody had the feeling we were not in control and we didn't like that. We were vulnerable to being bombed or otherwise attacked while we were under tow on the surface. We needed to be able to dive, surface and otherwise maneuver the ship. We felt we were trapped. Submariner's are like that. It made us nervous from that standpoint and the thought was always in the back of our minds. Most of us felt more secure when submerged. However we were happy to be heading home.

Life aboard the *Dolphin* was weird. It wasn't like a normal in-port duty situation and certainly not an underway watch. We stood watches topside to keep an eye on our little tug and make sure the tow lines hadn't parted. The Exec had a fire axe placed in the windlass room in order to cut the towing hawsers if we were attacked. We were still watching the skies for Japanese aircraft and the seas for enemy ships. A man with a sound powered phone was stationed in each of the seven compartments (the conning tower still could not be occupied due to the damage). He could take action and spread the alarm if any major casualty occurred. Clyde spent a good deal of his time stopping small valves from leaking. We were blessed with calm weather for most of the trip. Most of us had lingering emotional feelings about our baptism of fire in Kagoshima Wan. That feeling was to linger with me for many years to come.

We were blessed with calm weather for the rest of our trip. Mr. Bass allowed some of the men up on the wrecked bridge to see daylight every once in a while provided that they had life jackets available. An officer and one lookout were usually the only ones standing lookout on the bridge. About all we had to watch for in addition to the towing hawsers parting as we were being towed was the possibility of the tug suddenly stopping without warning. Our momentum might cause us to keep on going and possibly collide with the *Algorma*. Below decks there were but a few details that needed to be attended to, such as a daily clean sweep-down in each compartment. We needed to have our bilges as clean as possible in case we had a sudden leak and needed to start pumping. Generally we had to neaten up the ship. We had to have a semblance of order even though we were in such a shambles topside we needed to have the below decks areas presentable for the Admiral, the Squadron and the Division Commanders, if and when they came aboard. After all, we were still a U.S. Navy ship and we were proud of it.

At Midway we had received some fresh food and canned stuff like beef stew and tomato soup. About thirty gallons of fresh milk and some apples and oranges were included. It wasn't enough, but it gave us a welcome change for which we were grateful. The Motor Machinists were able to keep making fresh water because we didn't need to worry about using up diesel fuel. With our reduced crew we could take longer showers and that made us feel a better. We were thankful we had old "Belly Robber" Chuck as our cook. He could do wonders with powdered milk, powdered eggs and Spam. He even surprised us on Thanksgiving Day by serving a noon meal of chicken and dumplings with a side of canned cranberry sauce. There apparently were no turkeys at the commissary. He had hoarded as much of the fresh food we got at Midway, as he could, for this occasion. Without him the ten days to Pearl Harbor would have been grim in the food department.

Sully and the Motor Machinists, including Clyde, were working to get the engines back in commission. The electricians were busy finding and eliminating as many electrical grounds as they could find. We were a small but busy hive of worker bees and all of us were feeling good again, happy to be heading home. The Exec broke out the medicinal alcohol, little 2oz bottles of Bourbon, and allowed one drink for each man aboard at the evening meal each night. Clyde got ambitious and put the arm on the guys that didn't drink, such as me, and tried to persuade them to let him have their allotment. It worked and he amassed quite a store of the little bottles of liquor. I couldn't figure out when or where he would capitalize on his acquisitions. He never did to my knowledge. Somebody who took over later might have found out where he stashed them.

Our daily routine worked out well and the guys settled down to playing acey-deucy, back-gammon, or hearts. The officers had a bridge tournament that went on until we reached Pearl. Several of the chiefs who had remained aboard were assigned to OOD duties so the officers could keep their game going. Some of us wrote letters and others were content to play records on the ship's record player. Since Christmas was coming up a few of the men started thinking about devising some sort of Christmas cards but most of them decided we'd get back to Pearl in time to mail some good cards. One of the guys, "Mattress Back," seemed content with the situation. He was found to be putting in an extra amount of time sleeping in his rack in the after battery. I couldn't put Meilin out of my mind. I got out my writing gear and composed a brief note to her. I told her how I fondly remembered that day we had a picnic on the grounds next to the Royal and the band from the hotel played all that nice music while we were eating. I remembered our Teriyaki barbecued chicken and drinking our Ginseng tea. I apologized again for my sudden departure without calling her. I told her I missed her and her Eskimo type kissing. We were still too far from Honolulu to pick up their radio stations and get any world news.

Chapter X: Remember the Sabbath

The seasoned veterans remaining aboard ship had no lack of things to keep them busy. All sorts of bolts and nuts had to be tightened up by the Motor Machinists. Clyde had finally given up on trying to fix number one air compressor. The torpedo men were preparing the torpedoes for off loading when we got back into Pearl. The Electricians still worked on electrical circuits that needed to be replaced or rewired. The Radiomen continued correcting the problems with the circuits in the radio trunk which had grounded out. All of us were relieved to have the pressure removed of the possibility of the Dolphin not making it back to Midway. Now we were sure we were going to make it home.

The Motor Machinists finally got the second direct drive diesel engine back in operation but we were still down to one of the generator engines. The commutator ring on the out of commission generator engine had burned out and we had no spare rings to fix it. Both batteries had several cells that had to be jumped and isolated. Only one shaft could be used if we needed propulsion without the high pitched squeal of metal to metal.

We continued wallowing along behind the *Algorma* at about six knots. At dawn the next day we made a landfall on Kauai, Mount Kawaikini to be exact. The mountain, usually covered with clouds and rarely seen from the surface, has become known as one of the rainiest spots on the face of the earth. We all began to breathe easier now that the end was in sight. Home and family began to have a deeper meaning to me since our ordeal in Japanese waters. I'm sure most, maybe all of the rest of the crew felt the same way. Home was a good place to be. Home would be comfortable. I started to think about taking leave and getting back to visit my mom and dad in the San Francisco Bay Area. My father was in the photo finishing business in Berkeley and my sister was attending the University of California. I thought about finishing my letter to Meilin and maybe asking her to go with me to visit my family if I could get some leave. I discarded the thought. We would soon be back in Pearl Harbor and I could call her after we were tied up. I hoped I could get liberty and go see her. I knew I could at least phone her.

At 0830 we were passing between Niihau and Kauai and heading directly toward Oahu and everything seemed fine. With little watch standing to do we had been playing cards and other games. By this time we had picked up a radio station from Honolulu. It was playing the music most of the guys liked. "San Antonio Rose" was one of our favorites. Our spirits picked up some, but not for long. I was called up to the bridge when Mr. Ward called down to have a Quartermaster come to the bridge to read a message that was being directed at us. I was in the conning tower at the time and raced up to the bridge with the blinker gun. The blinker message was from the *Algorma*. It told us about the attack on Pearl Harbor and Honolulu. It was Sunday December 7, 1941. The message sent icy chills up my spine.

It quoted a plain language radio broadcast on the military frequency: "AIR RAIDS ON PEARL HARBOR. THIS IS NO DRILL."

Listening to Honolulu radio had given us no hint of any attack. Who was attacking? It slowly began to sink in. It had to be the Japanese. If that was the case, and it was, then what we had witnessed at Kagoshima was without doubt a full-scale dress rehearsal of this attack that Commander Minoru Genda, of the Imperial Japanese Navy, had masterminded. He disclosed this rehearsal in his book, *Tora, Tora, Tora*, in 1963.

Mr. Bass scrambled up on the wrecked bridge. We were

powerless. We couldn't mount a single 50 caliber machine gun and our 4 inch deck gun was inoperable. Even if it were operable it could be used only against surface targets, not aircraft. The *Algorma* flashed us another message.

"Am going to cast off the tow line. Urgently needed in P.H. You're on your own."

Mr. Bass told me to send a message back to the *Algorma*. Luckily I had the blinker gun on the bridge because our signal light had been destroyed off of Kagashima.

The message I sent read, "Negative cast off. Proceed best speed Pearl Harbor."

No response from *Algorma* for about five minutes. Finally their signal man blinked back a message: "Will come along side and secure you to our starboard side to facilitate entry to Pearl."

The tug's skipper was clearly alarmed and for good reason. Mr. Bass out ranked the *Algorma's* skipper and the Exec's seniority prevailed.

There were towering columns of smoke coming from many different places with the heaviest originating from the Pearl and Hickam field areas. By this time we could see airplanes all over Oahu. We were still too far away to identify if they were the attacking planes or ours. The radio gang got us tuned into the general circuit which was all in plain language. The voice messages were all garbled and disjointed. It sounded like complete panic. By this time Honolulu radio was also chaotic and reported bombing in the downtown part of the city. I began to worry about Meilin.

The *Algorma* signaled us to cast off the towing hawsers. When she had those aboard she came alongside and passed over lines that tied us fore and aft as well as spring or surge lines. Mr. Bass ordered all hands topside to wear life jackets while handling lines. We broke out our mooring lines from their deck lockers in anticipation of tying-up at one of the sub base finger piers. Electricians stationed in our maneuvering room were told to be ready to answer bells on the battery. The steering stand in the control room was untied and manned in case we had to be on our own. We were all set to be on our own by the time we reached Papa Hotel.

It was now 1300. A lone PBY came droning over us, looking as menacing as it could, but it didn't drop anything. It had to be obvious to them that we were just a Navy tug with a tow alongside. A destroyer, which turned out to be the *U.S.S. Ward (DD-139)*, came charging over toward us with a bone in its teeth and heavy black smoke pouring from all of its four stacks. It looked like it meant business. They challenged us. Blinker signals from the *Algorma* soon verified that both of us were friendly. The *Ward* directed *Algorma* to wait until she got orders from Harbor Control before trying to enter the channel. The *Ward* soon charged off in another direction presumably to look for Japanese submarines. The *Algorma* radioed Harbor Control and within fifteen minutes we got permission to enter. Now there were anti-submarine nets across the entrance which weren't there when we got under way on this patrol. Presently the nets were towed open and we proceeded into Pearl. The nets closed behind us. Harbor Control was really on the ball and seemed to be responding fast without any sense of panic. The panic we were hearing on the radio was now subsiding.

We were appalled at seeing the battleship *Nevada* aground on the north west side of the channel opposite Hospital Point. It appeared to be badly damaged and was smoking heavily. A harbor tug was alongside her spraying volumes of water on her after decks to help put out the fires. One of the new Fletcher class destroyers came charging down the channel heading out the channel toward Papa Hotel. It was making knots. They probably were going out to help the *Ward* look for enemy submarines, but who knows what they were going to do. I thought they certainly couldn't tackle a Japanese battleship or a cruiser. The Exec offered the opinion that with an attack this massive the Japanese could possibly have troop transports and make an attempt to invade Oahu. If so perhaps the Ward and the other destroyer we saw would at least try to attack them.

After passing the *Nevada,* we saw huge plumes of fire and smoke coming from Pearl Harbor Naval Shipyard to our starboard. Off our port bow you could see the leaning masts and the superstructure of the battle ship *California* with smoke and flames roiling up from below its decks. Looking past the *California* along battleship row we saw nothing but masts, derricks, and various parts of superstructures poking up through the billowing smoke. I saw the superstructure of my favorite Battleship, the *USS Tennessee (BB-43)*. It didn't look too badly damaged to me, but the *West Virginia's (BB-48)* smoke and obvious damage prevented my knowing whether or not the *Tennessee* was badly damaged. It didn't appear to have been sunk as did the *West Virginia.*

We were sickened by the carnage and destruction of those stalwart giants of our fleet. The rounded bottom of a capsized battleship, which later, I discovered, turned out to be the *Oklahoma*, looked obscene in the midst of all the other burning, shattered hulks. Not seeing the carriers moored off of Ford Island, I wondered if they had been sunk already.

By this time most of our crew were topside looking at this holocaust. You can imagine our thoughts at seeing this all but total destruction: rage and frustration. Anger demands revenge. We needed to do something, and yet we were powerless to do anything. We couldn't fire a torpedo or the deck gun. Without periscopes, even if we could submerge, we couldn't fire a torpedo. We were a warship unable to go to war. The only difference between the *Dolphin* and the rest of the wrecks around the harbor was that we weren't on fire or smoking. All of us topside experienced together the horrific shock at the devastation we saw.

Staring at this disaster, I wondered, had we returned a day or two earlier, would we have been able to prevent this carnage? Would enough people in the higher echelons of the Navy have listened to the *Dolphin's* report and been prepared for this onslaught?

General George Washington sent a message to the Continental Congress during the Revolutionary War emphasizing his plight at Valley Forge asking, "Is anybody there? Does anybody care?"

I was hoping some of the brass among the higher echelon was on top of this disaster and cared. I believed they did care and were taking action about it right now. The *Dolphin* had been there and seen the high level bombers bombing; the torpedo bombers dropping torpedoes. Now it became abundantly clear why we had heard no explosions from the bombs and torpedoes that we saw dropped at Kagoshima. In hind-sight they were clearly using the equivalent of our exercise torpedoes that had no explosives. We had seen of what Japan was capable, but were unable to radio the facts back to the Naval Scouting Force Commander, Pacific. We had a real clue. It was a preview of this attack and had we been able to get back sooner and tell the powers that be what we saw and experienced, would things have been different? I felt guilty about that. Not only because of the enormous loss of life at Pearl Harbor, but because the submarines in our fleet would have to learn what we had learned the hard way; by experience, if we couldn't share our experiences with them. I knew we would be called upon to do just that.

The *Algorma* headed us toward the 10-10 dock at the Navy yard, the closest place where there was a spot they could put us. The dock was 1010 feet long; thus 10-10 dock. It was normally reserved for the Pacific Fleet flagship; the *Pennsylvania* at this time but she was in drydock nearby. Motor launches and other small boats were scurrying all around the harbor picking up bodies as they spotted them among the multitude of debris. By this time, it appeared that there were very few survivors to be found, only bodies still floating in the leaden, oily looking water. The motor launches, normally clean with their brass fittings shining, had their hulls coated with the goo from the black Bunker-C oil coating the water. The small craft showed themselves to be aware of our presence. They got out of our way as we ploughed through the thick layer of oil heading toward the dock. Looking around we seemed to be just another piece of floating junk in a harbor full of floating and partially sunken junk. Our superstructure, especially the wrecked bridge, was bright orange from the rust. So much for the CRS bridge fair-water. Nobody paid any mind to us. We no longer had the sinister, dark, shark-like profile of a U. S. Navy submarine.

There were no line handlers available as the tug placed us starboard side-to the 10-10 dock. Our nose was pressed into the pier just ahead of the *Helena* and *Oglala*. The *Oglala* had capsized and the *Helena* was badly damaged. Our line handlers had to leap to the dock from the bow. The men scrambled, unsteadily, to grab the heaving lines we threw over to them and then they hauled in the mooring lines to tie us up. The *Algorma* quickly took in their lines and left at a high rate of speed. The trashed *Dolphin* made no noticeable impression on the sailors running frantically along the pier. Except for the lack of smoke, *Dolphin*, looked like the rest of the smoldering, ruined ships in the harbor.

Doubled up and secured with spring lines set, most of us were now topside staring in disbelief at the dense smoke and fires that were burning, everywhere. It seemed the smoke and flames, came from the Bunker-C oil from the ruptured fuel tanks of the capital ships that were sunk or badly damaged. The smoke had a smell I'll never forget. It was the smell of oil, gun powder and charred human flesh. It made us all sick to our stomachs. Nausea took on a new meaning for me. The skipper of the *Cachalot*, who was a classmate of Captain Malvern, saw the *Dolphin* being pushed in toward the 10-10 dock, and had hurried over. He wanted to see Captain Malvern. Mr. Bass, who was still on deck, climbed out on the dock, saluted him and shook his hand. They had a brief discussion and the skipper went back to his boat which was farther down 10 - 10 dock but out of sight. The *Helena* and the *Oglala*, were blocking our view..

Now I knew for sure that what we witnessed at Kagoshima was a prelude to this horror. It was apparently a full dress rehearsal for this attack. Had we returned a week or even a day earlier we could have alerted ComPacFleet; Admiral Kimmel. The armed forces on Oahu could been placed on higher alert. We had found that the Japanese were a formidable enemy which was preparing for a momentous operation. Maybe the fact that the Captain was the only one who actually saw the planes dropping their armament could have been suspect, but all of us experienced the depth charging. We knew about the Japanese destroyers being able to echo range. The top brass should have wanted to interview us. Our skipper and most of our crew were there five days earlier. Had they been interviewed? If not, why not? I hoped they were but if they were nobody had listened to what they had to say. With only one third of a submarine's officers and crew returning from a patrol without their skipper and a trashed submarine certainly should have given the top brass a wake up call. Why didn't it?

Mr. Bass went on the dock again and made a telephone call. Apparently the Naval base phone lines were still working. About a half an hour later a jeep drove down the pier and a couple of officers and a Yeoman got out. They took a look at the *Dolphin* but did not come aboard. They held a short conference on the pier with the Exec and Lt. Molloy. The Yeoman took some notes and the officers politely but curtly turned down an offer of a quick inspection tour of *Dolphin*. They left in a hurry. Mr. Bass came back aboard and told us we had to move under our own power over to the sub base finger piers. We got under way on the battery, and despite the squeal in the port shaft we made it to Sail Two, the closest finger pier. Sail Two was the same pier that we left from when we got underway on our special assignment. Sailors from the *Narwhal* on the other side of the pier took our lines in, helping tie us up. They appeared to be in shock at our condition. Thank God we didn't have a current or tidal flow to contend with on this move.

After tying up, the Exec told us to stand fast and stay aboard until he got back from Commander Submarine Scouting Force headquarters. We were helpless. Clyde ran across the pier to the *Narwhal* to see if he could get any dope. When he got back he told us the Army expected an invasion momentarily and had put every available soldier on the various beaches to man whatever machine guns that could be had. He said the Army had moved as many cannons as they could to positions where they might be needed to repel invasion forces including Wakiki. Clyde wanted us to break out our 50 caliber machine guns and be ready for the next wave of planes. I reminded him that we didn't have a stanchion left to mount the guns. He said he could weld one out of scrap pipe and headed below for the acetylene tanks and torches. Sully went to find some piping from the *Narwhal*.

There were three other submarines in Pearl that Sunday. The *Narwhal, Cachalot* and *Tautog. Tautog* had manned 50-caliber machine guns and was credited with shooting down a Japanesese plane. Pleased at that report I scurried over to the *Narwhal* to see a fellow Quartermaster friend of mine to get the straight scoop. He told me the *Cachalot* got strafed. It had a few bullet holes in it and one of their crew was badly wounded. He was the submarine force's first personnel casualty during World War II. The other two boats weren't hit at all.

The Exec came back telling us an all clear signal had been broadcast and we stopped trying to install the 50-caliber mounts. *Tautog* and *Narwhal* were standing at ease by their machine guns by now. Mr. Bass told us to secure the ship as best we could and remove all our personal gear off the boat. He said that he would meet with us on the third floor of the barracks first thing the next morning. We took off, leaving a topside watch and below decks watch. Mr. Holman remained as the only officer aboard. We bumped into several sailors we knew from other submarines. They were full of all kinds of scuttlebutt. They would say things like, "Did you hear that both the *Saratoga* and the *Enterprise* were sunk on the way back from Wake and Midway?" or "We heard that the *Lurline* was sunk as she was docking in Honolulu." All were wild rumors and here were many more.

Captain Malvern had not made an appearance but that didn't surprise me considering his condition when he left the boat at Midway. We assumed he had been taken to Tripler, an Army hospital, situated high on the side of the hills overlooking Pearl Harbor. They called Tripler "The Pink Palace" in those days. We used to say if you were ever sent to Tripler you would never be seen or heard from again. I knew some guys who were sent there. I never did hear about or from them again. The problem really was that the Army's paperwork was very different from the Navy's, and I know there was a lot of red tape in the various chains-of-command during those pre-war days. I'm sure no one was ever lost. I heard later the Captain had been placed in a mental case ward at Tripler. He was subsequently sent to an institution of some sort in the States. He retired from the Navy and died a few years after the end of the war.

Shortly after the attack the Navy took over the Royal Hawaiian Hotel in Honolulu. Admiral Nimitz, a former submariner himself, had the idea and ordered it done. The submariners returning from war patrols were comfortably ensconced there for two weeks of R & R. Because of its pink color and lavish decorations the submarine sailors quickly dubbed it "the Pink Palace". The term "Palace" was certainly appropriate when you considered that those sailors had just spent 30 to 60 days or more at sea confined in a relatively small, smelly sewer pipe of a ship. Tripler quickly lost that title.

We headed over to the barracks. On the way I noted that it looked like the diving tower had not been hit during the air raid. More importantly the diesel fuel tank farm on the hillside by the base wasn't bombed. That proved to be a real blessing in getting our submarines out to sea on their forthcoming long range patrols. As we walked up the pathway to the barracks we could see the barracks hadn't received any damage either. When we got up to the *Dolphin's* floor we found our fellow crewmen who had been flown back to Pearl from Midway were conspicuous by their absence. Their lockers were open, and empty. Their bunks had been stripped of their "fart sacks" (mattress covers). The bulletin board had been cleared off, even the thumb tacks were gone. Didn't they want the *Dolphin* sailors leaving messages for us? I got a strange feeling that all was not right.

I attempted to call Meilin but the outside phone lines were down or tied up with this emergency. I wanted to see Meilin and tell her that I was back and OK. I knew that she would be worried about me because of the attack. I felt that I needed to tell her about my feelings toward her. I wanted to unload some of my emotions from the *Dolphin's* patrol. She was a good listener. I also had some stuff in my locker at the YMCA that I wanted to retrieve. I knew that no sailors could go into Honolulu without liberty cards. We didn't have liberty cards so I went down to the *Cachalot*'s floor and found a guy by the name of Gallagher who was in the draft of men from New London to Panama. When I first got to Pearl I ran into him, renewing the friendship we formed in Panama. I asked him to lend me his liberty card if he wasn't going ashore. He said OK.

Without taking the shower which I so desperately needed, I shifted from my dungarees into my whites and headed for the Makalapa gate. When I got there I found I didn't need a liberty card or my whites. The guards told me that the buses were not running because of the attack and liberty cards were suspended. The guard also told me he was under orders not to let anyone in or out without official orders or were on official business even if he was in uniform. I wasn't going any where. I went back to the barracks and changed back into my dungarees. I tried to think of someway that I could wrangle a way to get out on some kind of official business. I wandered over to the gedunk stand near the Makalapa gate. A sub-base pick-up truck was there with its engine idling while the two sailors, I recognized from off of the *Tautog*, were getting a coke. I struck up a conversation with them. They knew I was off the *Dolphin* and said they were heading to Fort DeRussy at Wakiki to pick up some small-arms for the *Tautog*. I asked if I could go along. The driver said I could if I would help them unload back at the *Tautog*.

That was fine with me. On the way I asked if they could drop me off at the YMCA while they went for the small arms. The driver said it was no problem but warned me I had only an hour. If I wasn't there, they would go back without me. I knew for sure I couldn't take that chance. When we got to Honolulu it was a mess. Fire engines and police cars were going every which way with sirens blaring and lights flashing. There was pervasive, heavy smoke and lots of damage. People seemed to have gone berserk and were clogging the streets. Some had packs on their backs. Others were pulling carts piled up with belongings. It was a far cry from the laid back, sleepy, city I knew before leaving on our trip to Japan. The pick-up dropped me off at the Y across the street from the Black Cat Café. The Café had a large, crudely lettered sign saying, "Closed." I went to my locker in the Y and got my civies out. Why I did that I'll never know because I didn't have the time even if I could wear them.

I was starting to put them on when one of the other sailors at their lockers yelled at me, "Hey, sailor. You can't wear those civies."

"Why not?" I hollered back.

Why couldn't I wear my civies? The sailor didn't answer. He just looked at me as if I'd lost my mind. Then it hit me. And hit me hard. We were at war. Martial law had been imposed.

There was a phone in the lobby of the Y and I tried again to phone Meilin. The lines were down. It seemed Honolulu had been bombed too. Not just Pearl. We didn't know until later that much of the damage was from our own anti-aircraft shells that were fired at the Japanese planes. They didn't explode in the air, but the did when they hit the ground in downtown Honolulu. The result was 57 men, women, and children were killed.

On the ride into Honolulu I noticed all the shops along Beretania Street were closed so I knew Meilin wouldn't be there. I decided to hoof it over to her place, but I couldn't get there. There were bomb craters in the block where she lived and that scared the hell out of me. The situation didn't look good. I recognized the proprietor of the Chinese grocery store where Meilin shopped. In his coolie-like hat and pajamas he was running up the street. I yelled at him in Chinese. He stopped, remembered me after a moment. He started to tell me something in Cantonese but he was so agitated I had to tell him to slow down. He then reverted to broken English as he told me Meilin's apartment house was destroyed and that she had been one of those killed

Paul, who had been attentively listening to my story said, "Oh my God! Now I know why the Chinese hostess at Do Ho's startled you so much."

I pulled my wallet out of my pocket and removed a tattered picture of Meilin and showed it to Paul.

"That picture was taken at her father's house one Sunday in July 1941. I've carried it with me ever since then. I hope I still have a good copy in one of my albums."

"She was a pretty girl. I can see why you must miss her so much."

"She meant a lot to me. More than I can ever say. I never found out if she received the letter I asked Stark to mail for me from Midway. I hope she did."

Dazed and numb, I wandered back to the Y. Meilin had meant more to me than I was aware of up until that time. As I reached Beretania Street the pick-up truck was waiting for me. It had stopped and picked up some other sailors heading back to Pearl. Almost insensible, I quietly rode with them back to the base. The other passengers had show their liberty cards and their ID's to The guard at the gate . Since I was in dungarees they assumed I was with the *Tautog* sailors and I didn't volunteer anything different.

After helping unload the small arms as promised I headed for the barracks. Up on the third floor the guys greeted me with the news I was in deep trouble. The Exec was looking for me. They said they had lied, telling him I had gone to the dispensary for something. The Exec had gone over to the dispensary, found out I not only wasn't there but I had never been there. Things were looking blacker for me than ever. I thought after today and Meilin's death, what else can happen to me now?

Meilin was dead. She was all I could think about. She dominated my thoughts.

Chapter XI: The Scattering

At 1230 the remaining four officers and twenty men of the *Dolphin* were assembled on our floor of the barracks. Mr. Bass told us we were going to get a top secret briefing.

We asked the Exec where the other two thirds of the crew and officers were and his reply was simply, "I don't know."

I looked over at Mr. Holman and noted he looked pale. I wondered if he was as nervous as I was? All of us were confused and apprehensive. I am sure I was the worst because of Meilin's death. The men who smoked were puffing up a storm. A few of the younger guys were biting their fingernails. The tension was high.

At about 1315 a crusty looking Commander, a little on the heavy set side, appeared with a Ltjg walking in ahead of him. The faded gold scrambled eggs on the bill of the Commander's cap plus the three tarnished gold stripes on his shoulder boards were indicative he had been wearing that rank for some length of time. His rumpled uniform showed signs of having been worn for quite some time. He may have been recalled to active duty recently.

As he entered the room the Ltjg, wearing khakis with a black neck tie and the gold piping of an aide, on his shoulder at the top of his arm, called out, "Attention on Deck!" It was followed shortly by, "As you were."

Some of the guys stood up and some didn't. We weren't used to that kind of language. It was standard usage on a capital ship. Never aboard submarines. There was a saying aboard submarines that everyone leaves his rank or rate at the gangway as they came aboard except for the Captain. As they shut the door behind them, I caught a glimpse of an armed guard, with the SP band on his sleeve, standing outside. I assumed that he was to prevent entry to the room but maybe it was to keep anyone from leaving. Were we considered prisoners?

The Lieutenant announced, "Commander Nash has a few words to say to you."

His appearance was consistent with my recollections of the old automobile of the same name. He had a vintage appearance.

The Commander drew himself up to his maximum stature and asked with a snarl, "Lieutenant Bass, are all hands present now?"

I detected the implication that the meeting had been scheduled earlier but someone had been missing. Obviously, I was the one who had been missing.

"Yes, sir! With the exception of the officers and men who were flown in from Midway."

"Do I sense a touch of sarcasm here, Mr. Bass?"

"No, sir. I just don't know where the other officers and men are and I cannot account for them."

Mr. Bass's ruddy complexion had deepened.

My impromptu trip to Honolulu had certainly prevented an earlier meeting. They had required all hands present and I was not to be found. I had gotten off easy on that one.

The Commander stood staring at us for a long minute. I felt as if he considered us prisoners of war. He might have even considered us Japanese.

"You may sit down but don't get too comfortable. I want you to listen and pay strict attention to what I'm going to say. I'm going to say it as loud and as clear as I can."

There weren't enough chairs for all of us. Some of us stood, some sat on the edge of a bunk while others sat cross legged on the deck.

"Your trip to the waters of the Empire of Japan was just that. A trip. However, since you went into Japanese National waters, it was an illegal trip. That fact makes everything that happened Top Secret. Everything you did or saw is now Top Secret."

I wondered why the trip was illegal? That was not a Navy term. He sounded like a District Attorney in a court room.

Commander Nash paused and his eyes went from man to man. It made us feel very uncomfortable. He settled a stare at me for a minute. I was squirming and beads of perspiration were popping out on my forehead. We knew what we did could have been construed as an attack on Japan but we were now at war with Japan. I failed to see why our experience would make any difference.

"You are not to discuss this episode with any living being," the Commander continued. "You will not talk to any newspaper or radio people or any governmental agency."

He paused again as if to emphasize the significance of his words. He obviously wanted it to penetrate our minds.

"Lieutenant Livermore is handing out some forms I want you all to sign."

The Commander waited while we got the forms and signed them. I wanted to ask what would happen if we didn't sign the form, but I didn't have the guts. After all Mr. Bass, Mr. Molloy, Mr. Holman and Mr. Ward didn't ask any questions so why should I. I contemplated signing a phoney name to mine but realized that would be stupid. I wanted to ask for time to read the document completely but I didn't dare. The JG went through the room and picked up the papers from us, inspecting each one as he got it.

"Lieutenant, have the all the documents been signed?"

"Yes, sir, Commander."

"The document that you men just signed is the legal form that forbids you from ever talking publicly about what happened or what you did over the last three months. Now raise your right hands and swear you will never divulge anything about the *Dolphin's* patrol to Japan, to any person for the rest of your lives."

We swore and after we put our hands down, the Commander paused again. He looked each man in the eye and said, "The oath you have just sworn to must never, never be violated. Is that clear?"

Again, none of us asked any questions. The Commander was so stern and angry looking that none of us dared say or do anything. Someone high up in the brass had to have been deeply disturbed about the possible international repercussions of our patrol.

"You are all confined to the barracks until further notice and will not to talk to anyone about this meeting. You will not go to Ships Service or to the dispensary without my permission and then only one at a time. You will have chow in the mess hall after the base is served. You will not talk to the mess cooks. As far as you officers are concerned you will have your meals with the crew. You will not go to the Officer's Mess or the Officer's Club."

Puzzled by this, all we could do was to look at each other with questions in our eyes. We waited for the next bomb. At least the officers were able to bunk in the Bachelor Officers quarters for the time being.

"Each of you will receive orders that are being prepared at this time. Lieutenant Livermore will be here each morning at 0930 with individual orders as they become finalized. Lt Bass will be your contact with me if any problems arise until such time as you receive your orders. I trust each of you is now aware of the seriousness of this."

He paused and stared at us as if to make his message more indelible in our minds. He didn't ask us if we had any questions.

"That is all."

The Commander and his aide left the room and we were left in stunned silence and staring at each other. Before any of us could talk Mr. Bass spoke up.

"I don't know what I can say, men. We're all in this thing together. All this fuss may just be due to the general hysteria surrounding the Japanese attack on Pearl. I'm sure we will all make out all right and be properly assigned. They have to put together a skeleton crew while they consider what they have to do to the *Dolphin* so she can fight in this war."

We broke up into small groups and started to commiserate. Most of the guys had frowns on their faces. I know that I must have had one as I puzzled over the Commander's use of the word *"finalized"* in regard to our forthcoming orders. To me it had an ominous sound. I thought back for a moment to the flash of the blue-green light that I saw on our first evening at sea at the start of the *Dolphin's* first day underway. I wondered if the omen of St Elmo's fire had finally overcome my good luck omen? Paul, who was listening patiently to my story, interrupted,

"What happened then, Captain?"

We settled down into a dream like routine. We looked and felt like zombies. Like we were dead, yet still alive.

Two days later things started to happen. Among the first to go was Chief Brown. He managed to tell me, when we both were in the head at the same time, that his orders were to report to new construction at the Electric Boat company in New London. I heard later thEFat he was assigned as Chief-of-the-Boat of the *U.S.S. Amberjack* (*SS-219*). I'm sure that he had his hands full with the construction and commissioning details of that boat to the extent that he would have little or no time for reminiscing. Mr. Bass, was transferred to the *Plunger* which was en route to Pearl from Mare Island. I believe he made Lieutenant Commander and was in the Naval Academy class year group that was slated for command. I never found out whether or not he got command of *Plunger*. I hope he did. He was a damn good officer.

I learned many years later that Mr. Molloy became Captain of one of our boats that was sunk by the Japanese during the war. I don't remember which one. Mr. Holman, I found out, was sent to the New London Submarine base where he became an officer instructor. From there he became an officer on one of the new boats built by Electric Boat company. I believe it was the *USS Growler (SS-215)*. I lost track of Mr. Ward and the rest of the junior officers. They were a fine bunch of officers and I am sure they accounted for themselves in an appropriate manner where ever they were assigned.

As far as the enlisted men were concerned it was hard to track any of them down. I never knew where most of them went. I since found out Ding-Dong shipped out to Australia along with three others. I'm sure the four of them were assigned to different boats. Clyde went to an "S" boat in San Diego where he became chief of the boat. Sully was sent to a fleet boat in the Aleutian Islands. Others went to "S" or "R" boats in the Coco Solo Operating Base in the Panama Canal

Zone and the Key West submarine base in Florida . The lucky ones were assigned to New Construction at Mare Island Naval Shipyard or the new construction yard at Manitowoc, Wisconsin. Maybe even Portsmouth Naval Shipyard in New Hampshire. Curiously I noted no one was assigned to a school boat at either New London or San Diego. I wondered why? Maybe they didn't want any of us talking to the new volunteer submarine sailors.

Now that we were at war, the Navy had to beef up each available submarine by at least three officers and fifteen enlisted men. I believe that all the *Dolphin's* crew were sent to other submarines or became part of a pool of men that could be useful until they were needed aboard another submarine. This pool was later designated as a "Relief Crew." A number of such pools were established as the war increased in intensity. It became policy to transfer one third or about ten to twelve percent of each crew when their submarine returned from patrol, unlike the way they scattered the *Dolphin's* crew.

It seemed odd to me that none of our officers or crewmen were retained as a nucleus crew for our submarine after it came out of shipyard and was ready for sea again. Only a few of our men remaining had a clue as to the *Dolphin's* peculiarities and idiosyncrasies. It would be tough on any crew to take over our submarine not knowing, for example, of our high or main induction problems as well as the cranky MAN diesels. The potential was there for the loss of a vitally needed submarine in time of war coupled with the loss of a highly trained crew also in short supply during the first few months in 1942.

Some of the *Dolphin's* men were undoubtedly lost on other submarines that were sunk during the war. Others died of "old age" since those days leaving only a handful of us alive who could tell our story. The way we were scattered it surely took powerful logistics to assure none of the *Dolphin's* crew ended up on the same submarine or base and we were deprived of engaging in talk of the past. Plus the fact that each of us would have our own new adventures and dangers to face. Some of the guys could put everything behind them and forget the adventure that almost got all of us killed. I couldn't.

"Captain, what happened to you?"

"I was the last to go, Paul. It was like waiting for the other shoe to drop. Everyone else received orders and was gone within a week or so. I was going stir crazy. It was as if I had been placed in solitary confinement. I was still numb thinking about Meilin and what she obviously meant to me. I was unable to contact any of her family to offer my condolences. The only thing I could do was to read books and magazines and I got bored doing that. I did manage to sneak out to the base theater to see a movie. I don't remember its name because I was so nervous about being caught. I wanted to strike out at somebody or something even if it meant prison or death. I didn't care. I was angry. I hated the Japanese."

On December 17, I was ordered by Lt. Livermore to report to the Commander Nash's office. I was surprised because the Lieutenant didn't hand me orders as he did to all the others. I walked with him over to the Commanders sparsely furnished office. It was on the top floor of the administration building and had windows overlooking the finger piers of the sub base. You could look across Quarry Loch and see the shipyard with all the feverish repair activities going on. The only decorations in the room were an American flag and a framed picture of President Franklin D. Roosevelt hanging on the wall. The Commander was sitting at a standard navy grey metal desk strewn with paper. Propped up by an ink bottle was a colored photograph of a woman in a flowered dress with a small little girl about ten years of age. Presumably his wife and child. I thought briefly that the Commander couldn't be all bad if he had a family that looked like that.

The Commander did not look up as I entered his office. I stood there at attention and waited for what seemed to me about five minutes before he looked up. He did not invite me to sit down or even stand at ease. He was deliberately making me sweat. He had a scowl on his already stern face as he looked up.

"Swenson, You are in big trouble. We know that you stole a liberty card and tried to get out the gate. We know all about your AWOL foray into Honolulu allegedly to help pick up some small arms. You were confined to barracks. You lied to your shipmates when you told them you had to go to the dispensary. Everything you did was against orders. I'm authorized to administer nonjudicial punishment for these offenses."

The Commander paused and stared at me.

"You are hereby reduced in rate to Seaman second class. Thanks to your former Executive Officer, Lieutenant Bass, there is no forfeiture of pay. I wanted to give you a 'Convenience of the Government' discharge but I was talked out of it. However, it's better this way since we can keep tabs on you wherever you're ordered in the future. If you lose your senses again you'll find yourself breaking rocks at Leavenworth. You've shown a total disregard of authority and we're moving you out of submarines."

I looked him straight in the face as I felt a crimson flush rise on my face.

"Sir, I think that would be a terrible mistake. I have a valuable background in submarines. My offenses were not that serious and they were not what you may think they were."

"Your orders are already cut," he continued. "You'll proceed by government transportation to Naval Air Station, Olathe, Kansas. You will wear a uniform bearing your new E-2 rate. Here are your orders and itinerary and remember the admonition I gave you and your shipmates. Do not discuss your experiences to anyone at any time. Ever! Is that clear."

"Yes, sir!"

"Dismissed."

"But sir, I..."

"You – are – dismissed."

"Aye, aye, sir."

The Commander handed me my orders and looked down at his paper work and appeared to get immediately engrossed in his writing again. I did a military about face an left the room. I was in shock. I wasn't aware whether any of the other guys got busted. I had a clean record. I didn't deserve such severe punishment for such a minor and understandable incident. If they would only have let me tell my story

I would have felt a lot better.

Paul rose up from his chair, looked at me intently for what seemed minutes and after a brief pause said, "Captain, I have to go to my room for a minute. I'll be right back."

"OK, Paul, but hurry. I don't want to drink alone and shouldn't especially in my current frame of mind."

Paul returned about a half hour later looking serious.

"What's that look on your face mean, Paul?"

"Captain. I made a quick call to my contacts at Naval Archives and found out something that ties into what you just told me. All records for the *Dolphin* are missing for October, November and December 1941. They couldn't tell me why."

"I think I know the reason. They're still uptight about the *Dolphin's* patrol, Paul. I finally figured out why they don't want to let out any part of the story."

"Spill it, Captain!"

"I think Admiral Kimmel and his staff were reading between the lines of the intelligence they did get and suspected that something was being kept from them. It didn't take too many smarts to figure out other possible targets of the Japanese. Since then, I've personally been on strategic planning boards in which we analyzed situations and looked for possible alternate objectives."

"Captain, if that's true, it might shed some light on the Husband–Kimmel controversy."

"I think it does, Paul. It has weighed heavily on my mind for some time."

"Wouldn't someone on the staff have spoken up?"

"I don't think so. Staff officers as well as Junior officers are reluctant to buck the tide. They think of their own careers and keep that sort of stuff under their hats. The top brass would be afraid to disclose that they had a real clue to the impending attack on Pearl Harbor and that the mission they sent the *Dolphin* on was too little, too late. The Admirals could be held at fault for trying to determine what the Japanese were doing on their own and possibly exposing what we knew from the code breakers. We had broken the Japanese Flag Officer codes before the attack. They likely were afraid that it would cause political embarrassment to the Executive Branch of the government and to the two top military men both Army and Navy. They had to hide the blame for whatever intelligence break down there might have been. I have often wondered if the code breakers had found any records of the Japanese attacking a submarine in their waters during that time frame. It may have been before they had broken the codes and it may have been in plain language and they didn't attach any significance to it."

"Captain, don't you think they should have released what you went through to their subordinate commands?"

"Sure. Both surface and subsurface. We learned a whole lot of things that should have been reported to the first boats going on patrol after the attack on Pearl that Sunday. We could have warned them about the pinging ability of the Japanese destroyers. They needed to know that the Japanese aircraft could very likely home in on the SD radar and to use it sparingly. We could have told them to weight down their garbage. We might have warned them about the time it takes your eyes to dark adapt from the lighting in the conning tower, or below decks, to the pitch black on the surface. And what about having the contour lights removed? The fact that torpedo storage racks could have poor or failing catches and other serious problems needed to be looked at.

"The small boats we carried were not desirable or needed. They were useless and awkward to handle. The access ladder built in to the superstructure was not necessary and rattled a lot. They would learn all that quickly. A critical problem plaguing the later boats was that the torpedoes stored in topside deck containers could develop hot runs. Especially the boats that had external torpedo tubes built into their superstructure. They were one shot tubes and when the torpedo was fired they couldn't reload them. Also the torpedoes they carried in those tubes couldn't be serviced while at sea. There is no record as to any malfunctions of those torpedoes."

"Why wouldn't they want the other boats to know these things?"

"Paul, it might have led to questions such as 'How did you find that out?' and 'Who told you?' "

"Wow! I can see why you're worried."

"I don't believe that I'm in any trouble at this time, as long as you don't spill all this to anyone."

"You can trust me, sir."

"At least I feel a little relieved now that I got the story off my mind."

"If you don't have any strong objections, Captain, I would like to call Senator Martin and ask him to give a look into this without mentioning any names. I'd like to ask him to find out if the secrecy of something this old is still necessary. I'll see if there is really anything to fear. It may have been just an oversight when they enacted the Freedom of Information Act."

"Paul, I trust you but, please be very careful what you say. It could possibly spell trouble for me and for you, personally, if you are too aggressive in your investigation."

"Captain. I'll be very careful."

"Well, I spilled my guts to you Paul and now I have to accept the consequences no matter how all this turns out."

"It'll take a while to get through to the Senator so I may be a while."

"Paul, it's late anyway. To paraphrase Scarlett O'Hara in *Gone with the Wind*, Let's think about it tomorrow. Good night."

"That sounds good to me, Captain. I'll call you tomorrow morning. Good night."

Paul left the room, leaving me to muse about what I had just done. At age 81, there are not too many years left for me anyway. I poured myself a double scotch and tried to erase the visions that my talk with Paul had evoked. Perhaps Porky and Ding-Dong were the sane ones and I was off my rocker. Over the years I had buried all thoughts about the *Dolphin* mainly because I had become intent on being the best submarine officer I could be.

At one time when I was a Division Commander during the Cold War, I sent one of my boats out on an intelligence gathering mission that could have been extremely hazardous. The *Dolphin's* assignment came to mind briefly but I reasoned that the *Rock*, then being in good repair and recently out of the Naval shipyard, would stand a relatively good chance. As it turned out, the hazards didn't materialize and the *Rock* returned safely much to my relief.

The next morning, after showering and shaving, I dressed in shorts and an aloha shirt and started feeling better. I had breakfast alone, early. I wanted to avoid both Carl and Paul. I didn't want to talk. In the middle of eating my cereal and Papaya fruit who should show up? None other than Carl.

"Good morning, Captain. I hope everything went OK with you and your friend yesterday. You left the base in a hurry. Is anything wrong?"

"Morning, Carl. I was just reminded of a bad experience I had many years ago and I had to collect my thoughts for awhile. I think I have things under control now. Care to sit down and join me while I finish my breakfast?"

"Thanks for the invite, Captain, but I am supposed to meet I guy I served with over in Rota, Spain for breakfast."

"Fine, Carl. Maybe we can catch up with each other later today or tomorrow."

"See you."

I headed back to my room at the Hawaiian. Yesterday's cathartic spilling of my guts to Paul left me feeling exhausted and edgy. Whatever sleep I got didn't relax me or give me any feeling of well being. At approximately ten o'clock the phone rang. It was Paul. He said that he'd like to come down in about an hour. He said that he had some news for me. In a short time there was a knock on the door. I opened it and Paul greeted me with a big smile.

"What's that grin on your face mean, Paul?"

"Good news! Captain, Senator Martin looked into this thing for me and just now called me back. He said that there's no reason to worry. Your signature on that document you signed was obtained under duress during a time of heightened emotions and therefore is null and void. The Senator added that sometimes things are done under the guise of 'National Security' when the real reasons are political. This could be why it was quietly swept under the rug."

"It still sounds as though I might need a lawyer if this gets out."

"According to Senator Martin, the reason the *Dolphin* was chosen for this mission, was probably that it was the only submarine available for a National Security Agency task without attracting any undue attention. If it were lost, it wouldn't have been a big deal. If the Japanese had sunk the *Dolphin* and attacked Pearl Harbor soon afterward, the whole episode might never have been exposed and nothing would need to be covered up. The *Dolphin's* personnel would have been listed as having been killed in the attack on the Naval base. Senator Martin said that since we had broken the Japanese codes before the attack it is possible that Admiral Kimmel didn't get one or two of the key messages that would have changed his actions."

"I had heard that Admiral Kimmel had orders to conserve fuel oil, probably Bunker-C, and therefore kept the bulk of the fleet in port instead of sending some to sea to support the carriers that were transporting fighter aircraft to Wake and Midway. But I can't rely on rumors like that, Paul."

"The Senator said he was going to try to find out who actually ordered the *Dolphin* out on this mission."

"Oh, oh! That may spell trouble for me, Paul."

"I don't think so, Captain. He doesn't know I am talking about you or any other *Dolphin* sailor. He said the secrecy of your patrol was suspicious in the first place because all navies reconnoiter other countries all the time."

"I'm quite aware of that aspect. I have done my share of 'off shore' reconnaissance operations since then."

"Then that implies there may have been a conflict of interest between the Administration and the Commander of Naval Forces Pacific, doesn't it?"

"That's right. "I've been speculating about that for many years. At least every time I am reminded about the *Dolphin's* patrol."

"Senator Martin also said that the secrecy surrounding the Pearl

Harbor attack has long ago subsided and it would only come up if one political party thought they could embarrass the other by pointing fingers. He said as long as there is no potential for the story to get into print you can rest easy."

"Rest easy? Rest easy? Paul, it makes me feel as though I was on the table in Edgar Allen Poe's *Pit and the Pendulum* story. As far as I'm concerned, the pendulum is still swinging and it's getting closer. I haven't many years left and I'd like to live long enough to enjoy what time I do have."

"I know Senator Martin is a fighter. He'll go to bat for you if necessary."

"He may never know a problem exists until it is too late, Paul."

Paul's good news message did not ease my mind a bit. All I have to do is relax and hope Paul doesn't let it slip at a cocktail party or other function where liquor might cause him to lower his guard. He might tell someone my story and reveal his source.

"Paul, I wish I hadn't attended this convention. I know it'll take some time for me to sleep soundly again. I survived the non-judicial punishment and still achieved most of my career objectives. My misadventures didn't end with my exile to the Naval Air Station at Olathe, Kansas. I was lucky to get back into submarines later in the war. I was plagued with other problems on other submarines and some of them had the same implications of violation of international law that the *Dolphin* had. I witnessed two different mutinies by the officers on one submarine. I'll bet you never heard of any mutiny on any submarine. Right?"

"No I haven't. Were you involved in one?"

"Only in a peripheral way, Paul, but that's another story. Other situations I have experienced had to do with submarine commanding officers who were not able to cope with actual warfare. During the Korean War, I almost had to blow the whistle on a skipper who fully expected World War III would break out while we were on patrol in northern waters. He believed he would become a hero when he came back to port with a broom lashed to the top of the periscope shears indicating a clean sweep of the enemy from the seas. The *Dolphin's* episode was merely the beginning. It is hard to believe that I survived my experience on the *Dolphin* just to face more hair-raisers. I guess that I'm a survivor by nature, and if I live long enough, I could tell you a hell of a lot more."

Paul left the room and I was left to myself with my thoughts. Have I said too much? Did I talk to the right man? Will my efforts and achievements go down the drain? Perhaps I should change my will and specify my ashes be scattered over the Pacific Ocean near Honolulu just as the crew of *Dolphin* was scattered in December 1941.

The End of the Tale

Epilogue

At the time of this story the *Dolphin* was home ported in Hawaii and in the year prior to the Japanese attack on Pearl Harbor was sent on simulated war patrols that were of relatively short duration of two to three weeks. The places they reconnoitered were Midway Island and Wake Island. At some point during this period of international tension a senior officer of the Submarine Scouting Force was heard to say that any simulated war patrols to places other that Midway or Wake, and in particular, the Empire of Japan would be provocative and forbade them. Japan and Germany had recently signed the Anti-Comintern pact which said that if any of these countries was attacked the others would come to its aid.

After the Japanese attack on Pearl Harbor, *Dolphin* was immediately readied for war, provisioned and armed. On December 24, 1941 she was sent to the Marshall Islands. The poor condition of this old submarine plus the tensions they faced had apparently taken its toll on the Skipper, Gordon B. Rainer, (Naval Academy class of 1935). He apparently had a nervous break down midway during their first patrol which lasted forty two days. His executive officer informally relieved him of command for the remainder of the patrol. Upon reaching Pearl Harbor LCDR Rainer was sent to Trippler Army Hospital apparently for observation and a physical examination. When completed, he returned to the submarine base where he received orders to report to new construction at an East Coast yard. When he failed to show up at the appointed time attempts were made to find him. He was located about a month later wandering around in New Orleans. He seemed to be suffering from amnesia and was taken to Saint Elisabeth Hospital in Washington, D.C., near Bolling Air Force base. He was confined there for a period of time and retired from the Navy in 1943. He died in 1957.

A new Commanding Officer, Royal L. Rutter, (Naval Academy class of 1930) was appointed as commanding officer and patrolled off of Midway on its second patrol (15 days). At the conclusion of patrol number two after a brief refit, *Dolphin* was sent on patrol number three (68 days) in the waters off the Empire of Japan. A fourth patrol (51 days) was performed in the Aleutian Islands area. An analysis of all the *Dolphin's* patrol reports lead to the conclusion that she was not fit for combat. She was then relegated to serve as a training submarine at Pearl Harbor under the command of George G. Molumphy, (Naval Academy class of 1931). Medal of Honor recipient, Lcdr. D. W. Morton, (Naval Academy class of 1930) later the skipper of the famous submarine, *Wahoo,* had been assigned as Commanding Officer of the *Dolphin.* He turned down the appointment and is said to have made the comment that the *Dolphin* was a death trap Sometime later she was sent to New London to relieve the antiquated "O" boats of their submarine school duties. *Dolphin* provided a relatively modern platform for these duties and served well in this capacity until the end of the war.

The Naval shipyards as well as civilian yards made extraordinary progress in modernizing the submarines coming in from patrol during the war. They continued to bring them up to current standards as the war progressed. Many submarines of the same class did not resemble each other after various shipyards altered their configuration based on recommendations of Skippers completing war patrols.

Appendix I

THE V-7 CLASS - SPECIFICATIONS

Length Overall & Maximum Beam: 319' x 27'-11".
Displacement: 1,718 tons surfaced; 2,240 tons submerged.
Maximum Operating Depth: 250'.
Hull construction:: Partial double hull, riveted. ½ -inch thick plate.
Watertight Compartments: 8 plus conning tower and windlass room.
Crew: 7 officers, 3 chief petty officers, 53 men.
Torpedo Tubes: 4 bow, 2 stern.
Torpedo Load: 18 internal, 3 external.
Deck Gun: 1 - 4-inch 50 caliber.
Speed: Surfaced - 17 knots.
   Submerged - 8 knots for 1 hour.
Submerged endurance: 10 hours at 7 knots.
Range: 6,000 miles at 10 knots; 16,000 miles at 7 knots.
Endurance: 75 days.
Propulsion: Surfaced diesel-direct plus diesel-electric with 2 main engines and 2 generator engines. Submerged two 120 cell storage batteries driving two main electric motors plus two creep motors.

Appendix II

DOLPHIN (SS-169)

Shipyard: Portsmouth Naval Shipyard
Length: 319 feet
Displacement: 2215
Keel laid: June 14, 1930
Launched: March 8, 1932
Commissioned: June 1, 1932
First Commanding Officer: LT. John B. Griggs (USNA-19)
Stricken: 1946

Glossary of Terms

Angle on the bow-The angle from a targets course measured in degrees of arc to port or starboard of the bow of the target.

Automatic Pilot-Electro-mechanical control of a ships steering.

Battle stations-Places assigned each officer and enlisted man when the ship is going into action, submerged or surfaced (gun action).

Blow main ballast-Using high pressure air (3,000 lbs) to force water from the ballast tanks.

Bubble-The bubble of air in the inclinometer indicating an up angle, down angle, or zero angle.

Bullnose-A type of hawse pipe set on top of the bow for use of mooring lines or a tow line.

Christmas tree-The red or green lights on the board in the control room to indicate, when green, all hull openings are shut and it is safe to submerge. A red light would indicate that a valve or hatch was still open.

Compensation-Calculating the necessary amounts of water between trim tanks and in and out of the trim tanks in order to achieve diving trim or neutral buoyancy.

*Diving trim-*The condition of the submarine is so balanced that when submerged it will be close to neutral buoyancy and a horizontal (fore and aft) level trim.

*Fathom-*Six feet. It is the measure of depth in many countries. Its derivation, based on an ancient custom of measuring a fathom of rope by the spread of the arms. This action is strikingly like a home coming sailor greeting his sweetheart. From the old Anglo Saxon "faeom" meaning to embrace or grasp.

*Fathometer-*A sonic instrument which determines depth based on the time it takes a sound wave to travel from the ship's bottom to the ocean floor.

*Feather-*The visible wake of a periscope on the surface of the water.

*Flood-*To fill ballast or trim tanks with water from the sea.

*Fuel ballast tanks-*Tanks that carry fuel for increasing operating range. When empty of fuel they may be converted to main ballast tanks, providing additional freeboard and thus improving surface speed.

*Height of Eye-*The distance in feet that the observer's eye is above the water when taking the altitude of a celestial body.

*Hull down-*A ship sighted on the horizon with only mast showing.

*Inclinometer-*A level mounted in the control room which indicates the fore-and-aft attitude of the ship. The bubble in the level, if up, means the ship has an up angle.

*Main ballast tanks-*Main ballast tanks when empty provide for the required amount of air to maintain buoyancy to keep the submarine afloat.

Negative tank-a variable tank that when full provides negative buoyancy as well as imparting an initial down angle when submerging.

Ping-An audible signal from an active sonar

Planes-Moveable planes extending horizontally from both the bow and stern of the ship. The bow planes are normally folded up against the super structure when on the surface.

Planes man-The crew member assigned to operate the bow or stern planes controlling the ship's attitude when submerged.

Quick dive-Rapidly submerging while running at high speed.

Radar-A system of radio ranging and detection. A radio signal is transmitted, it meets an object and returns as an echo. The time these pulses require to go out and return gives an accurate determination of distance.

Range-The distance in yards from the ship to a target.

Safety tank- a main ballast tank that is used to compensate for a flooded conning or other partially flooded compartment in order to bring the conning tower above the surface.

Scope-Short for periscope.

Sonar-Underwater detection gear used by both surface ships and submarines. Active sonar can echo range and when an echo is received the distance of the contact can be calculated. Passive sonar can only be used for listening.

Stadimeter-An optical range finding device usually incorporated in the periscope.

Variable ballast tanks- used to maintain a satisfactory trim while submerged by transferring water from one to another and in and out to sea.

011 43 15 15 77 82